PAPERCUTZ™

MORE GREAT GRAPHIC NOVEL SERIES AVAILABLE FROM

PAPERCUTZ™

COMING SOON

THE ONLY LIVING BOY #1
"Prisoner of the Patchwork Planet"

THE ONLY LIVING BOY #2
"Beyond Sea and Sky"

THE ONLY LIVING BOY #3
"Once Upon a Time"

THE ONLY LIVING BOY #4
"Through the Murky Deep"

COMING SOON

HARDY BOYS ADVENTURE #1
"To Die Or Not To Die?"

THE ZODIAC LEGACY #1
"Tiger Island"

THE ZODIAC LEGACY #2
"Power Line"

THE ZODIAC LEGACY graphic novels are available for $7.99 in paperback, and $12.99 in hardcover. THE ONLY LIVING BOY graphic novels are $8.99 in paperback, and $13.99 in hardcover. HARDY BOYS ADVENTURES graphic nnovels are $15.99 in paperback only. Available from booksellers everywhere. You can also order online from www.papercutz.com. Or call 1-800-886-1223, Monday through Friday, 9–5 EST. MC, Visa, and AmEx accepted. To order by mail, please add $4.00 for postage and handling for first book ordered, $1.00 for each additional book and make check payable to NBM Publishing. Send to: Papercutz, 160 Broadway, Suite 700, East Wing, New York, NY 10038.

HARDY BOYS ADVENTRUES and THE ONLY LIVING BOY graphic novels are also available wherever e-books are sold.

HARDYBOYS ADVENTURES™

SCOTT LOBDELL – Writer
PH MARCONDES, DANIEL RENDON, SIDNEY LIMA – Artists
BASED ON THE SERIES BY
FRANKLIN W. DIXON

PAPERCUTZ™
NEW YORK

TABLE OF CONTENTS

TABLE OF CONTENTS

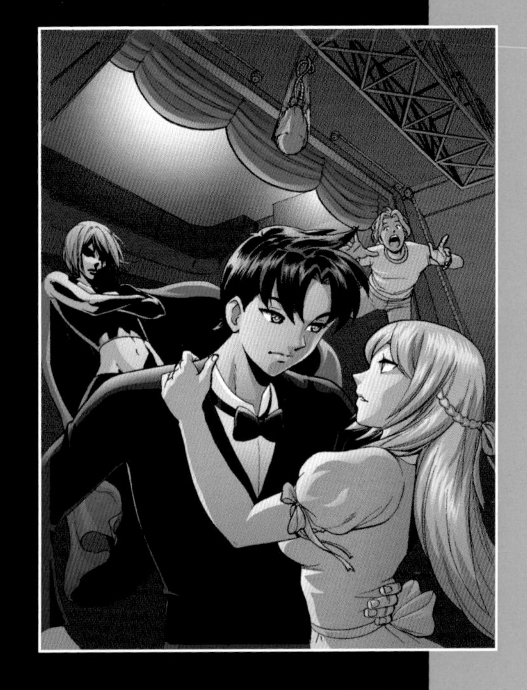

THE HARDY BOYS ADVENTURES #1

"The Opposite Numbers," "Board to Death," "To Die or Not to Die?" and "A Hardy Day's Night"

SCOTT LOBDELL – Writer
PH MARCONDES – Aritist, "The Opposite Numbers", "Board to Death," "To Die or Not to Die?," "A Hardy Day's Night"
DANIEL RENDON – Artist, "The Opposite Numbers"
SIDNEY LIMA – Artist, "The Oppostie Numbers"
MARCEL ZERO – Artist, "A Hardy Day's Night"
LAURIE E. SMITH – Colorist
MARK LERER – Letterer
DAWN GUZZO – Production
JEFF WHITMAN – Production Coordinator
SHELBY NETSCHKE – Collection Editor
JEFF WHITMAN – Assistant Managing Editor
JIM SALICRUP
Editor-in-Chief

ISBN: 978-1-62991-607-1

Printed in China through Four Colour Print Group
November 2016 by Shenzhen Caimei Printing Co., Ltd.

Distributed by Macmillian
First Printing

‘THE OPPOSITE NUMBERS...”
DON’T MOVE A MUSCLE.
I WON’T. BUT PLAYBACK HERE IS ANOTHER QUESTION.
THIS IS BAD! SQUARK THIS IS BAD!

CHAPTER ONE:
"PLEASE DON'T FEED
THE ANIMALS!"

IF WE HAD EVEN A MOMENT'S DISTRACTION, WE'D BE ABLE TO TURN AND MAKE OUR WAY THROUGH THIS GRATE.
WHAT'S DAD'S EXPRESSION?
"AND IF WISHES WERE FISHES NO ONE WOULD EVER GO HUNGRY."
WISHES SQUARK FISHES!

NO, JOE--
SEE WHAT HE'S
DOING?
PLAYBACK, NO!
PLAYBACK
IS CAUSING A
DISTRACTION
ALLOWING US
TO ESCAPE!
THAT'S ONE
SMART BIRD.
REMIND ME,
I OWE HIM A
CRACKER.
CRACKER
SQUARK
CRACKER!
GRRRRR!

SWIPE
SQUARK!

THAT WAS CLOSE!
AUNT TRUDY WOULD HAVE OUR HEADS IF ANYTHING HAPPENED TO PLAYBACK.
CHIRP.
WE'VE FOUND THE RARE ANIMALS AND BIRDS THAT HAVE GONE MISSING IN BAYPORT THIS PAST WEEK.
BUT WE STILL NEED TO FIND THE PEOPLE RESPONSIBLE.
IT'S ALMOST A GOOD THING THAT PLAYBACK HAD BEEN BIRD-NAPPED--
--OR WE WOULDN'T HAVE KNOWN ABOUT THIS CRISIS.
SHHHH, JOE.
VOICES COMING ROM BELOW.
SQUARK.
SHHH, PLAYBACK.

WE'RE GOING TO MAKE A BUNDLE ON THESE ANIMALS WE STOLE FROM THE ZOO AND OTHER PLACES.
YEAH, EXCEPT FOR THAT STUPID PET STORE PARROT. WHO'S IDEA WAS THAT?
TOMMY'S!

ME? I HATE THE DUMB BIRD!

LET'S TAKE THESE BOZOS DOWN, GUYS.
GRRRR.
LET'S. BUT MAYBE THERE'S A SIMPLER WAY.
CRACK

YANK

WHIIRRRRRRRRRRRRR
WHAT THE--?!
KIDS! GET THEM!

UM, FRANK. THERE'S A REASON YOU GAVE UP THE ELEMENT OF SURPRISE?
HMMM.

WHOA!
WHAT'S HAPPENING?!
WHHHIRRR
HUH?!
DUMB BIRD SQUARK DUMB BIRD!
HE TRIGGERED THAT PULLY--
--AND NOW WE'RE TRAPPED!
YOU NOTICED THAT NET UNDERNEATH THEM?
YOU'RE GOOD.

SOON...
MOMMY!
THANK YOU, BOYS! I WAS AFRAID I'D NEVER SEE PLAYBACK AGAIN!
IT WAS AN HONOR, AUNT TRUDY.
AND NOW THE OTHER ANIMALS ARE RESCUED TOO.
A MOMENT, BOYS?
CRACKERS FOR EVERYONE!
WE KNOW THIS WASN'T AN A.T.A.C.* ASSIGNMENT, DAD.
IT MIGHT SEEM A LITTLE TRIVIAL COMPARED TO OTHER STUFF WE'RE ASKED TO DO.
*A.T.A.C. :AMERICAN TEENS AGAINST CRIME.
ACTUALLY, I WANTED TO CONGRATULATE YOU BOTH ON A JOB WELL DONE.
NOT EVERY CASE YOU SOLVE HAS TO BE FOR THE TEEN SPY ORGANIZATION I HELPED FORM.
SOMETIMES IT'S JUST ABOUT DOING THE RIGHT THING.

Chapter Two: "Aaaaallllll aboard!"
BAYPORT HIGH SCHOOL, IN THE TOWN OF BAYPORT.
A PLACE WHERE NOT MUCH IS HAPPENING.
UNLESS YOU'RE A STUDENT PREPARING TO CELEBRATE...
BRNNNGGG
SPRING BREAK!
AND NOT A MOMENT TOO SOON!
I'LL SAY! MY HEAD WAS GOING TO EXPLODE FROM STUDYING.
OH, CHET YOU'RE A HOOT.

SO, DO YOU HAVE ANYTHING EXCITING PLANNED FOR THE NEXT TWO WEEKS?
I'M OFF TO A FOOD-TASTING CAMP.
A WHAT?!
IT'S ALL VERY SCIEN-TIFIC.
I WAS GOING TO USE MY FREE TIME TO DO SOME VOLUNTEER WORK WITH PROJECT SUNSHINE.
HOW...NICE.
I'M GOING TO BE MAKING PODCASTS OF MY NEW ALBUM.
CAN'T WAIT TO HEAR IT!
AREN'T YOU TWO GOING HOME ON THE BUS?
WE'VE DECIDED TO WALK HOME.
WE WANT TO START OUR MINI-VACATION WITH A BREATH OF FRESH AIR.
LATER!
BYE!
HAVE FUN!

WOW.
DO YOU HEAR THAT?
HEAR WHAT?

NOTHING.
NO GUNSHOTS.
NO SCREAMS.
NO SCREECHING TIRES.

HEH.
NO ALIBIS.
NO MOTIVES.
NO CONFESSIONS.

I LOVE THE WORK WE DO AS "UNDERCOVER BROTHERS," BUT--
BUT ONCE IN A WHILE IT'S FUN TO JUST RELAX AND BE NORMAL.
I HEAR YOU.
EXACTLY.

LATER...
THANKS FOR THE LIFT, DAD, BUT WE WERE ENJOYING THE WALK HOME!
SOMETIMES I FORGET THAT THIS TOWN IS SO BEAUTIFUL.
IT'S FUN TAKING THE SCENIC ROUTE.
I FEEL LIKE I'M SEE-ING BAYPORT FOR THE FIRST TIME.
LIFE'S LIKE THAT, JOE.
WE DON'T ALWAYS NOTICE WHAT IS RIGHT IN FRONT OF US.
HA! WE SEE YOUR POINT, DAD!
"BOARD TO DEATH"--AN A.T.A.C. ASSIGNMENT CAR-TRIDGE.
LOOKS AS IF WE'LL HAVE TO INFILTRATE A SKATE-BOARD COMPE-TITION.
SOUNDS LIKE A BLAST.

I GUESS WE BETTER GET PACKING.
DRESS LIGHT. THE CLUES ON THE BOX POINT TO CALIFORNIA.
HOLD UP A MOMENT, BOYS.

EVER SINCE YOU BRAVELY AGREED TO JOIN THE SECRET CRIME-FIGHTING AGENCY I CREATED--
--YOUR LIVES HAVE BEEN ONE NON-STOP ADVEN-TURE AFTER THE NEXT.
IT'S AN HONOR, DAD.
WE'RE ALWAYS PREPARED TO DO OUR SMALL PART.
THAT'S APPRECIATED, BOYS. MORE THAN YOU KNOW.
BUT YOU HAVE AN ENTIRE WEEK OFF UNTIL THIS ASSIGN-MENT--

WHICH IS WHY I WANT YOU TO TAKE YOUR TIME GETTING THERE.
TRAIN TICKETS TO CALIFORNIA?!
ON THE SILVERADO BULLET TRAIN?! WILD!
YOU TWO WILL BE MAKING THE TRIP IN THREE DAYS, WITH STOPS ALONG THE WAY.
IT WILL BE A GREAT OPPORTUNITY TO GET A GOOD, UP-CLOSE LOOK AT THIS COUNTRY YOU'VE HELPED SO MANY TIMES.
THANKS, DAD--YOU'RE THE BEST.
IT'S THE LEAST I COULD DO AFTER WHAT ALL YOU BOYS HAVE DONE.
SLEEPER CARS AND EVERY-THING. CLASSY.

THE NEXT MORNING...
...AT THE BAYPORT TRAIN STATION...

FRANK, DO YOU THINK DAD KNEW WE WERE JONESING FOR SOME DOWN TIME?
HE IS THE SMARTEST MAN I KNOW-- LET'S LEAVE IT AT THAT.

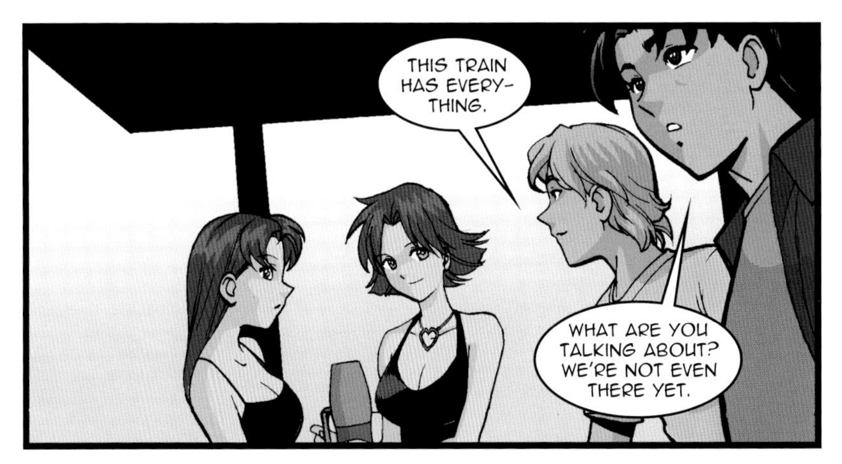
THIS TRAIN HAS EVERY-THING.
WHAT ARE YOU TALKING ABOUT? WE'RE NOT EVEN THERE YET.

NOW... WE'RE HERE.
I CAN ONLY THINK OF ONE WORD...

...AMAZING.

OH, NOOOOOOOOOOOO OOOOOOOOOOOOO OOOOOOOOO!
IT CAN'T BE! IT CAN'T BE!
CHAPTER THREE:
"TICKETS PLEASE!"
THAT SPEEDING TRAIN?!
IT'S NOT STOPPING!
THE TRAINS ARE GOING TO COLLIDE!

RUN!
WE'RE DOOMED-- DOOMED!
IIIEEE!
THERE ARE SO MANY PEOPLE BETWEEN US AND THE SWITCHING TOWER!
RIGHT IDEA, JOE!
COME ON, FRANK!
HUNH?
WRONG DIRECTION!
THIS WAY-- IT'S A SHORTCUT!
BRILLIANT, BRO!

ON ONE?
ONE!
WE ONLY HAVE SECONDS TO STOP THIS DISASTER!
A CALM HEAD ALWAYS PREVAILS.
BUT LET'S HURRY ANYWAY.

THE SWITCHING AGENT HAS PASSED OUT!
HMM.

THERE ARE A DOZEN SWITCHES HERE!
WE WON'T HAVE TIME TO THROW EVERY ONE!
HMM...

JOE--FLIP SWITCH 23-12, FROM SOUTH TO EAST.
I HOPE YOU'RE RIGHT...!
HOT STUFF

"NOW, JOE!"
"SWITCHING, FRANK!"

"AMAZING, FRANK! HOW DID YOU KNOW?!"
THE SCREENS COORDINATE WITH THE TRACKS AND LEVERS.
YOU'D HAVE BEEN ABLE TO FIGURE IT OUT.
YEAH, IN ABOUT A MONTH!
URRN...

LATER...
THAT POOR SWITCHING AGENT, HE CLAIMS HE JUST PASSED OUT.
YOU SAY "CLAIMS."
DOES THAT MEAN YOU DON'T BELIEVE HIM?
I GUESS THAT SOUNDS SUSPICIOUS, HUH?
MAYBE I'M SEEING A CASE WHERE THERE IS NONE.

THANKS FOR SAVING OUR BACON, HARDY BOYS!
DON'T MENTION IT, SIR.
WE'RE HAPPY WE COULD HELP.

WELCOME TO THE DINING CAR.
YOUR MEAL IS ON US!
THIS TRAIN GETS MORE IMPRES-SIVE WITH EVERY STEP!
I TOLD YOU IT HAD EVERYTHING.

FRANK! JOE!
YOU SIMPLY HAVE TO SIT WITH US!
SHIRA, SHHH!
SIT DOWN!

YOU TWO SAVED THE TRAIN-- WE ALL KNOW WHO YOU ARE!
I'M SHIRA NOIR, AND THIS IS MY LITTLE SISTER, NICOLINA.
SHE'S A LITTLE SHY AROUND BOYS.
SHIRA!
I KNOW THE TYPE.

WE JUST MET THIS WOMAN OURSELVES.
THIS IS TRE GELBMAN--HER JOB IS FASCI-NATING.
IT'S REALLY NOT THAT EXCITING.

I'M JUST A TRAVEL WRITER, RESEARCHING A BOOK.

IF YOU KNEW THE HISTORY OF TRAIN TRAVEL, YOUNG LADY--
--YOU'D BE AWED BY THE POWER OF THE LOCOMOTIVE.
THIS IS BRETT LOUIS, A TRAIN BUFF.
PLEASE, MR. LOUIS, ENLIGHTEN US.

AND SO IT GOES...
STRANGERS BECOME FRIENDS AS THEY TALK AND SHARE...

...WAY INTO THE NIGHT.
WHAT A GREAT GROUP OF PEOPLE.
IT'S KIND OF RELAXING TO JUST GET TO KNOW SOMEONE WITHOUT ASSUMING THEY ARE A SUSPECT FOR ONE CRIME OR--
OHHHHHH, NOOOOO OOOO!
HE'LL BE KILLED! HE'LL BE KILLED!
WHAT IS IT, MA'AM?!
CAN WE HELP YOU?
N-NOT M-ME!
THROUGH THAT D-DOOR...!

OH, NO! THE CONDUCTOR'S FALLEN FROM THE TRAIN!
IF NOT FOR HIS POCKET WATCH...!
IT'S BROUGHT HIM THE PRECIOUS SECONDS WE NEED TO ACT!

I'LL LOOK FOR A ROPE, OR SOMETHING WE CAN USE TO--
CHAPTER FOUR:
"I FEAR THAT TRAIN A' COMING!"
NO TIME!
HANG ON TO SOMETHING!
ANYTHING!

OH, MY!
I'D AGREE, MA'AM--
--BUT HE'LL BE FINE!
SO LONG AS I DO MY PART!
I GOT HIM, FRANK!
YANK US BACK ON "THREE"!
ONE...
...TWO...

...THREE!
EXCUSE US, MA'AM.
THAT WORKED OUT BETTER THAN IT HAD A RIGHT TO.
NEXT TIME, CAN YOU TAKE A FEW MOMENTS MORE TO COME UP WITH A PLAN?
I CAN TRY!

WHAT HAPPENED HERE?
JOE, FRANK--ARE YOU ALRIGHT?
WE HEARD THE COMMOTION...!
I'VE NEVER SEEN ANY SUCH THING! THESE TWO YOUNG BOYS RISKED THEIR LIVES TO SAVE THE CONDUCTOR!
MEDALS! THEY SHOULD GET MEDALS.
REALLY, IT WAS NOTHING.

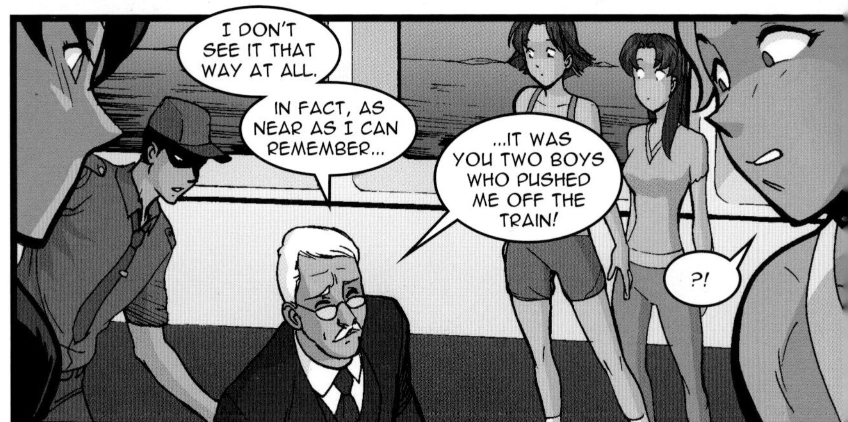
I DON'T SEE IT THAT WAY AT ALL.
IN FACT, AS NEAR AS I CAN REMEMBER...
...IT WAS YOU TWO BOYS WHO PUSHED ME OFF THE TRAIN!
?!

YOU'LL UNDERSTAND THAT I NEED TO HOLD YOU TWO UNTIL WE SORT THIS OUT.
NO OFFENSE, SIR--BUT THIS IS CRAZY.
BUT OF COURSE WE'LL COOPERATE.
WHAT'S THAT OLD SAYING? "NO GOOD DEED GOES UNPUNISHED."
WE WERE IN OUR SLEEPER CAR WHEN WE HEARD THE SHOUTS FOR HELP.
CAN YOU PROVE THAT?
HMM. THAT MIGHT BE A LITTLE HARD TO DO.
MAY I SUGGEST WE ALL CHECK THE TRAIN'S SURVEILLANCE CAMERAS?
THE WHAT...?
THERE, IN THE SHADOWS... THEY'RE ALL OVER THE TRAIN.
THAT'S MY SISTER! SHE DOESN'T MISS A THING!

MOMENTS LATER...
SECURITY
I PULLED UP THE RECORDED IMAGES FROM JUST BEFORE THE INCIDENT--
AND PUT BOTH VIDEO FEEDS ON THE SAME SCREEN.
COOL.

THIS IS THE HALLWAY WHERE THE HARDY BOYS WERE BUNKING DOWN
AND THIS IS THE EXTERIOR OF THE TRAIN.
SO FAR, SO CALM.

"WHOOPS! THERE'S THE CONDUCTOR--
"--LOOKING AS IF HE'S BEEN PUSHED!"

THERE THEY ARE--JUST EMERGING FROM THEIR SLEEPER CAR IN RESPONSE TO THE SCREAMS FOR HELP.
SO THEY COULDN'T BE RESPONSIBLE FOR WHAT HAPPENED.
SORRY ABOUT THAT, BOYS. I HAD TO MAKE SURE.
I KNEW IT!
YOU TWO ROCK!
NOT A PROBLEM, OFFICER.
AW, YOU WOULD DO THE SAME FOR US.

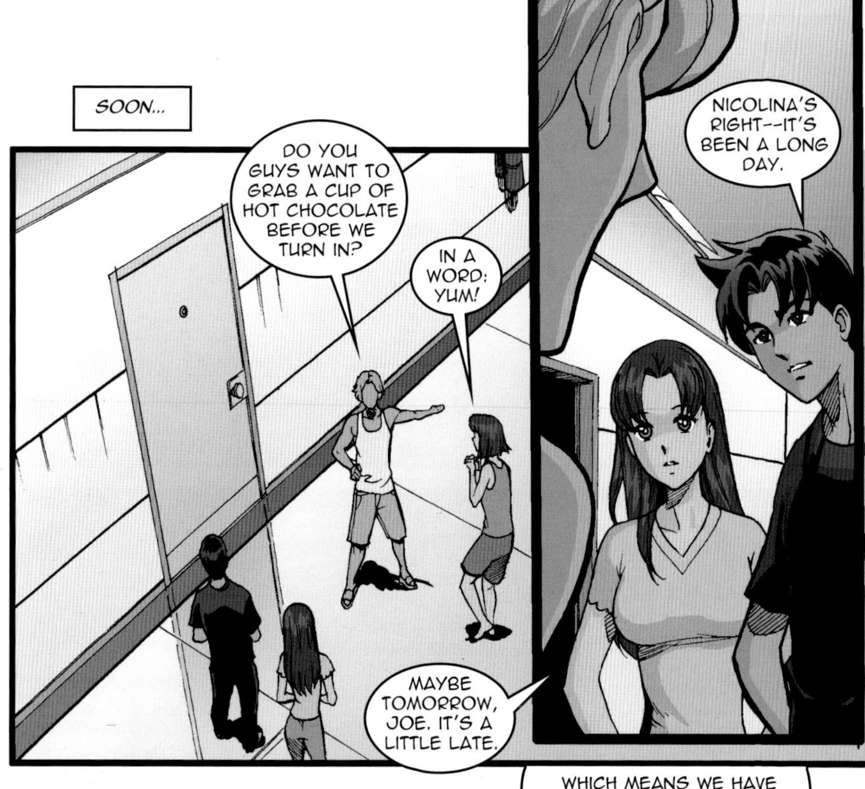
SOON...
DO YOU GUYS WANT TO GRAB A CUP OF HOT CHOCOLATE BEFORE WE TURN IN?
IN A WORD: YUM!
MAYBE TOMORROW, JOE. IT'S A LITTLE LATE.
NICOLINA'S RIGHT--IT'S BEEN A LONG DAY.

FRANK, I KNOW YOU'RE A LITTLE ON THE SHY SIDE, BUT--
IT'S NOT THAT, JOE. IT'S PRETTY CLEAR TO ME...
...THERE MAY BE A MURDERER ONBOARD.
WHICH MEANS WE HAVE A CASE TO SOLVE BEFORE SOMEONE GETS HURT.
YOU'RE RIGHT.
WE'VE BEEN WORKING FOR A.T.A.C. SO LONG, I DIDN'T EVEN NOTICE A CASE FELL INTO OUR LAPS.

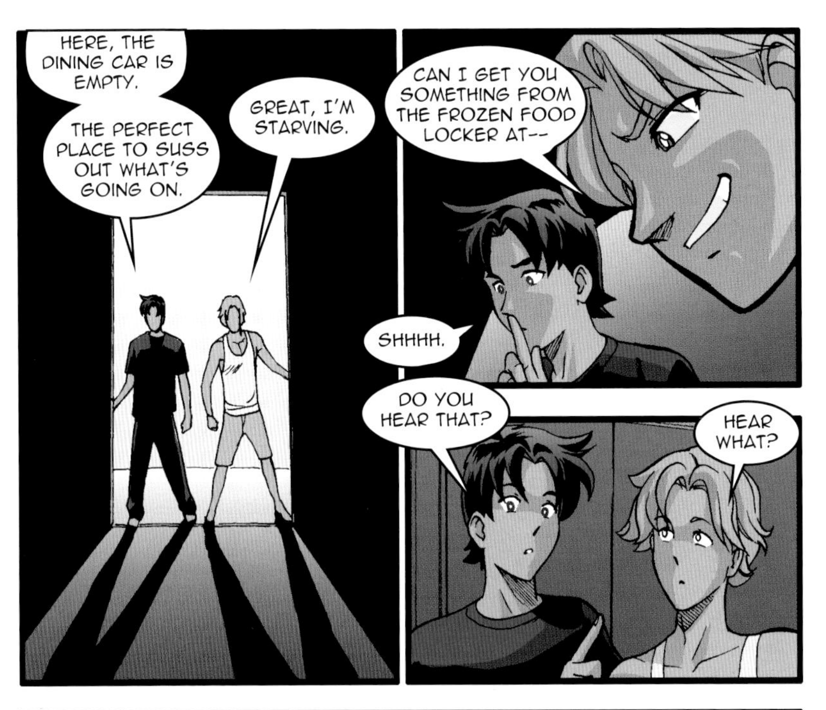
HERE, THE DINING CAR IS EMPTY.
THE PERFECT PLACE TO SUSS OUT WHAT'S GOING ON.
GREAT, I'M STARVING.
CAN I GET YOU SOMETHING FROM THE FROZEN FOOD LOCKER AT--
SHHHH.
DO YOU HEAR THAT?
HEAR WHAT?

'ELP ME...
IT'S COMING FROM THE FOOD LOCKER!

UH OH, THIS LOOKS BAD!
WORSE THAN BAD. AT THIS TEMPERATURE...
...BEING TRAPPED INSIDE THERE IS DEADLY!
P-PLEASE...

DON'T WORRY, TRE! WE'LL GET YOU OUT OF--
FRANK, IT'S LOCKED!
WE HAVE TO DO SOMETHING QUICKLY--SHE WON'T LAST LONG IF WE DON'T!
MAYBE THERE'S A WAY WE CAN CUT THE POWER TO THE LOCKER WHILE WE TRY TO FIND SOMEONE WITH A KEY?

CHAPTER FIVE:
"DEATH-WITH EXTRA ICE!"
OR IT MIGHT BE POSSIBLE TO PICK THIS LOCK..BUT IT MIGHT TAKE TOO LONG.
NO TIME! FRANK?

MOVE!
MOVING.
AND NOT AN INSTANT TOO SOON!
CLANG
DON'T WORRY, TRE-- WE'RE HERE!
TH-THANK Y-YOU.
LET'S GET HER OUTSIDE BEFORE HYPOTHERMIA SETS IN.

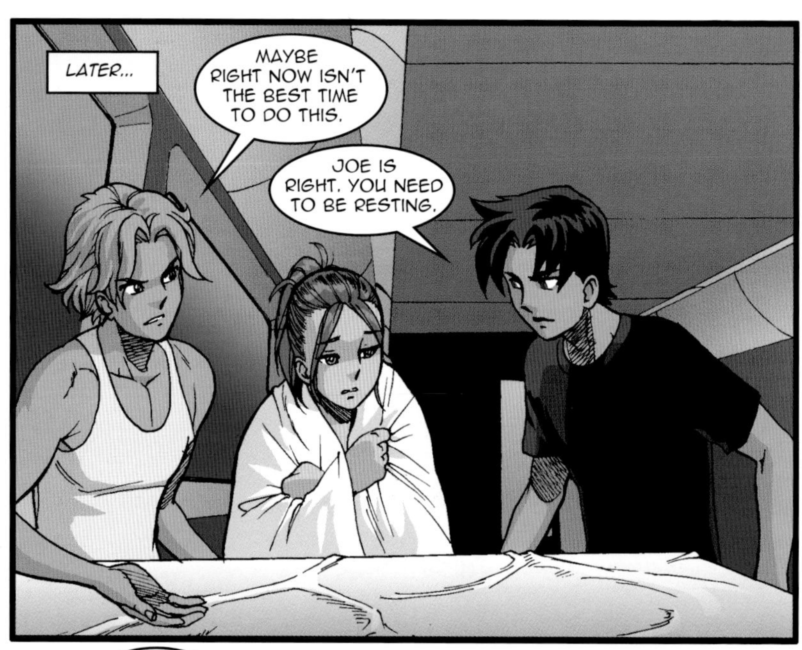
LATER...
MAYBE RIGHT NOW ISN'T THE BEST TIME TO DO THIS.
JOE IS RIGHT. YOU NEED TO BE RESTING.

HERE YOU GO, LITTLE LADY
THANK YOU, MR. LOUIS.
FUNNY HOW YOU TWO BOYS WANT TO PUT OFF QUESTIONING MISS GELBMAN.
I'LL TELL YOU SOONER THAN LATER IF IT CAN HELP YOU FIND THE PERSON RESPONSI-BLE.
I CAME DOWN HERE FOR A LATE NIGHT SNACK...
...WHEN SOMEONE ATTACKED ME FROM BEHIND.

AND THEN THE HARDY BOYS ARRIVE AT THE SCENE OF A CRIME. A MITE SUSPICIOUS, EH?
HEY! WHAT ARE YOU TRY-ING TO SAY?

YOU'RE TALK-ING NONSENSE, MAN. THESE TWO YOUNG MEN ARE HEROES.
THAT'S TOO MUCH, BUT THANK YOU, SIR.

DID YOU MISS THE PART WHERE THESE TWO SAVED MY LIFE?!
THAT'S TWICE NOW WE'VE BEEN SUSPECTS FOR A CRIME WE DIDN'T COMMIT!

I'M NOT GOING TO TAKE YOU IN, BOYS. BUT TRY TO STAY EXTRA FAR AWAY FROM TROUBLE?
LET'S SEE YOU SAFELY BACK, YOUNG LADY.
THANK YOU, GENTLE-MEN.

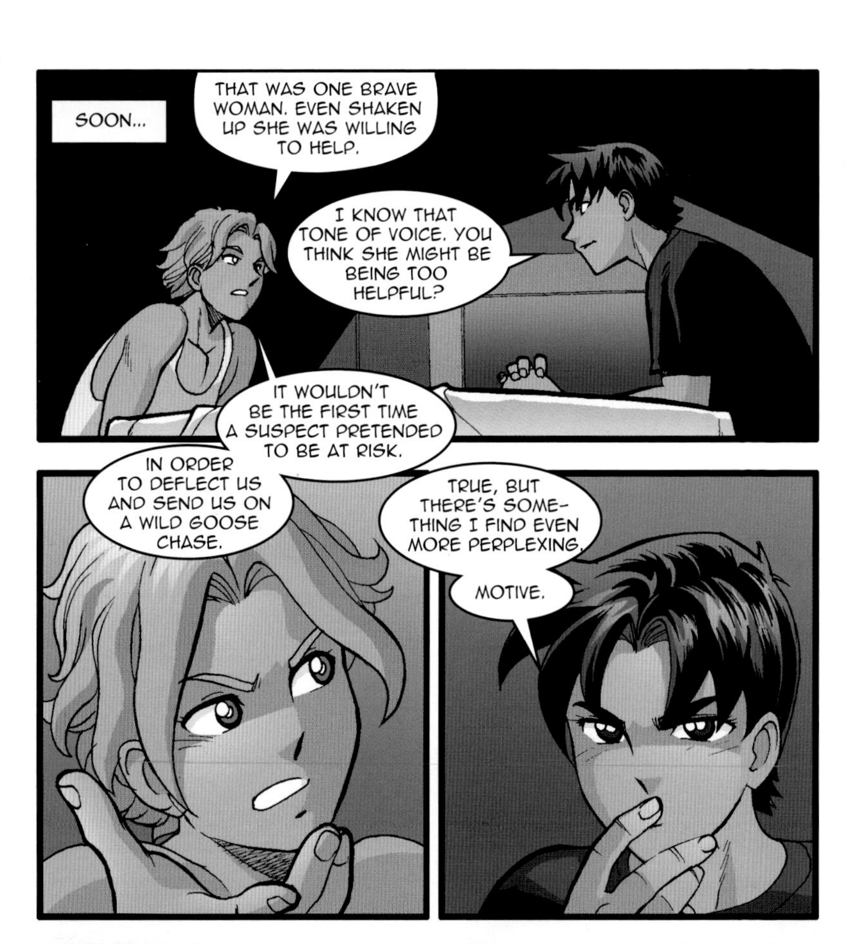
SOON...
THAT WAS ONE BRAVE WOMAN. EVEN SHAKEN UP SHE WAS WILLING TO HELP.
I KNOW THAT TONE OF VOICE. YOU THINK SHE MIGHT BE BEING TOO HELPFUL?
IT WOULDN'T BE THE FIRST TIME A SUSPECT PRETENDED TO BE AT RISK.
IN ORDER TO DEFLECT US AND SEND US ON A WILD GOOSE CHASE.
TRUE, BUT THERE'S SOME-THING I FIND EVEN MORE PERPLEXING.
MOTIVE.

SOMEONE IS TRYING TO CAUSE ONE CATASTROPHE AFTER ANOTHER...
...BUT WHY?
MAYBE IF WE CAN FIGURE THAT OUT, IT WILL LEAD US TO THE WHO.

HOME, SWEET HOME.
FOR NOW.
THIS "VACATION" IS GETTING TO BE MORE EXHAUSTING THAN AN ACTUAL CASE.
I'M BRUSHING MY TEETH THEN PASSING OUT LIKE THE PROVERBIAL LIGHT.
YOU WANT TOP BUNK OR BOTTOM?
TOP IS FINE.
JOE!
THIS ISN'T GOOD.
000
TIC
TIC
TIC

BOOM
DUCK AND COVER, JOE!
THAT WAS CLOSE!
CHAPTER SIX:
"DON'T LET THE BED BUGS... KILL!"

WE'RE NOT OUT OF DANGER YET!
COFF COFF
SMOKE FROM THE BLAST!
STAY LOW TO THE FLOOR--THE AIR IS BETTER THERE!

IT WOULD BE A DRAG IF WE SURVIVED THE BLAST BUT DIED OF SMOKE INHALATION.

AT LEAST WE'RE SAFE...
...FOR NOW.
"SAFE" BEING A RELATIVE TERM IN THIS CASE.
CH-CHOCK

I AGREE--
THIS SITUATION SHOULD NOT BE ESCALATING!
HUH?

NOW, IF WE CAN ALL TAKE A MOMENT AND CALMLY EVALUATE WHAT HAS HAPPENED?
ME? I'M HAPPY WITH JUST BUSTING SOME HEADS. JOE?
SORRY, I'M WITH FRANK ON THIS ONE.
WE'D BE BETTER OFF POOLING OUR RESOURCES IN AN EFFORT TO FIND THE PERSON RESPONSIBLE FOR ALL THIS CHAOS.
OR PERSONS!

FRANK, JOE... RUN!
WHA-- ?!
SHIRA?!
I'LL HOLD HIM BACK AS LONG AS I CAN! GET AWAY, GUYS!
I'M SORRY YOU GOT INVOLVED IN THIS, MISS!
CH-CHOK
YOU ARE ONE TRIGGER-HAPPY GUARD!
ENOUGH!
YOU?!

I AGREE-- THIS SITUATION SHOULD NOT BE ESCALATING!
HUH?

NOW, IF WE CAN ALL TAKE A MOMENT AND CALMLY EVALUATE WHAT HAS HAPPENED?
ME? I'M HAPPY WITH JUST BUSTING SOME HEADS. JOE?
SORRY, I'M WITH FRANK ON THIS ONE.
WE'D BE BETTER OFF POOLING OUR RESOURCES IN AN EFFORT TO FIND THE PERSON RESPONSIBLE FOR ALL THIS CHAOS.
OR PERSONS!

I DON'T TRUST ANYBODY AT THIS POINT!
I DIDN'T BUY A TICKET JUST TO GET IT PUNCHED IN THE MIDDLE OF NOWHERE!
ONE MORE MOVE AND I START SPRAYING LEAD--IS THAT CLEAR?
Y-YOU'RE NOT AUTHORIZED TO H-HOLD THAT GUN, M-MA'AM.
WHICH WON'T MAKE US ANY LESS DEAD IF SHE FIRES IT.
I SUGGEST WE ALL CALM DOWN AND--
SHUT UP! I'M THROUGH WITH CALMING DOWN!
I WANT ACTION AND I WANT IT NOW!
CH-CLAK

EMERGENCY BRAKE
ACTION IT IS THEN...
CHAPTER SEVEN: "THEM'S THE BRAKES!"
SCREEEEEEEEEEECH
THE EMERGENCY BRAKE?! GOOD THINKING, JOE!
...MA'AM.

BUMP

B-BUMP

FR-BUMP

OUCH.
WHAT IN SAM HILL?!

EXCUSE ME, SIS!
SHIRA?!
I NEED TO SEE A LADY...
ABOUT A GUN.
THANK YOU.
THERE YOU GO, OFFICER.
I'D LIKE TO SEE THE HARDY BOYS PULL OFF A MOVE LIKE THAT!
SPEAKING OF WHICH...!
I KNEW THERE WAS SOMETHING I DIDN'T TRUST ABOUT THOSE TWO!
THEY ESCAPED THROUGH THAT TRAP DOOR!

I FEEL LIKE WE'RE TAKING THE EASY WAY OUT.
HA! ONLY YOU WOULD THINK CLIMBING UNDER THE TRAIN IS THE EASY WAY OUT!

ONE FALSE MOVE AND WE'RE DONE FOR, JOE!

HERE--ANOTHER TRAP DOOR. LET'S SEE WHERE IT LEADS US.

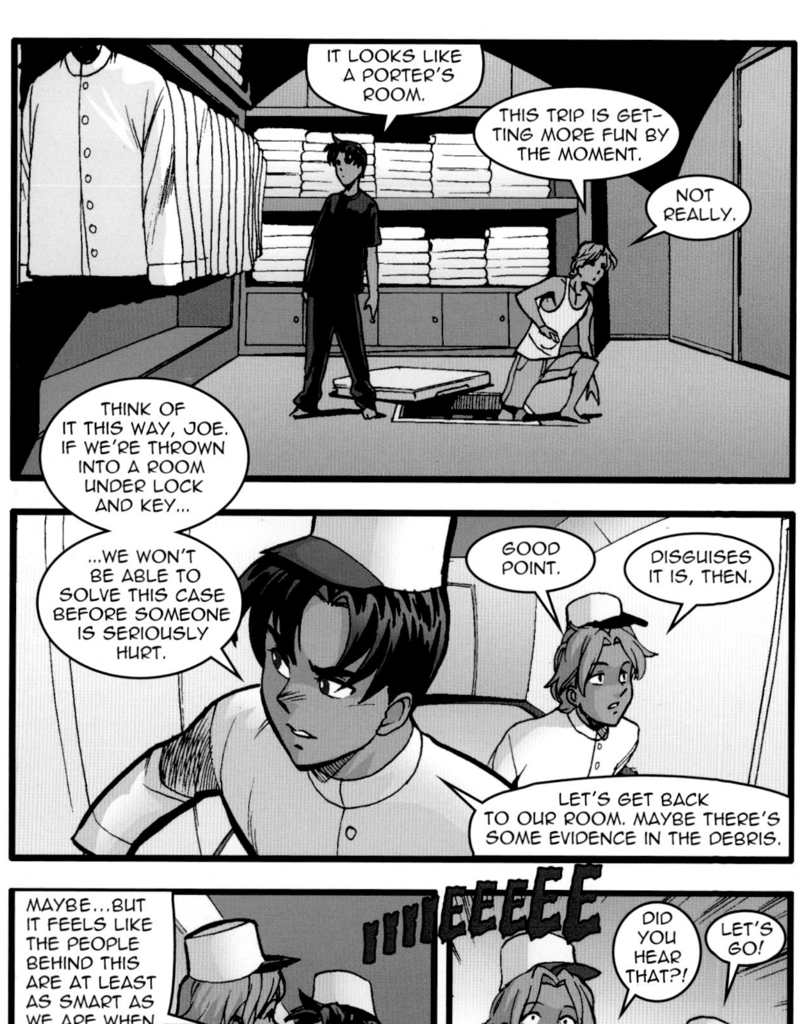
IT LOOKS LIKE A PORTER'S ROOM.
THIS TRIP IS GETTING MORE FUN BY THE MOMENT.
NOT REALLY.
THINK OF IT THIS WAY, JOE. IF WE'RE THROWN INTO A ROOM UNDER LOCK AND KEY...
...WE WON'T BE ABLE TO SOLVE THIS CASE BEFORE SOMEONE IS SERIOUSLY HURT.
GOOD POINT.
DISGUISES IT IS, THEN.
LET'S GET BACK TO OUR ROOM. MAYBE THERE'S SOME EVIDENCE IN THE DEBRIS.

MAYBE...BUT IT FEELS LIKE THE PEOPLE BEHIND THIS ARE AT LEAST AS SMART AS WE ARE WHEN IT COMES TO--
IIIIEEEEEE
DID YOU HEAR THAT?!
LET'S GO!

IT'S LOCKED!
STAND BACK!
KICK

MR. LOUIS?!
HELP!
THIS ISN'T YOUR CONCERN, GENTLEMEN!

CHAPTER EIGHT: "RUNNING OFF THE RAILS"
WE DON'T SEE IT THAT WAY, SIR.
ARE YOU OKAY?
I AM NOW-- COFF, COFF THANK YOU, SO MUCH!

YOU TWO ARE MAKING QUITE A HABIT...
...OUT OF RESCUING ME.
IT'S OUR PLEASURE.
I'M ONLY SORRY YOUR LIFE KEEPS GETTING THREATENED.

I WANTED TO TEACH HER A LESSON, ABOUT GIVING SOMEONE A BAD REVIEW!

BE THAT AS IT MAY, THAT'S NO REASON TO WANT TO KILL EVERYONE ELSE ON THE TRAIN.

"KILL EVERYONE ON--" ?!
I DIDN'T HAVE ANYTHING TO DO WITH THOSE OTHER INCIDENTS!
I MIGHT FEEL SLIGHTED ABOUT MY BOOK, BUT I'M NOT A MADMAN!

THE TRUTH IS, IT WAS A LITTLE BORING.
HERE'S AN EXAMPLE:
TRAINS OVER THE YEARS
"IN 1923, THE SPEED TRAP WAS DECOMMIS-SIONED. IT WAS VERY SAD. EVERYONE WAS SAD. IT WAS A GOOD TRAIN."

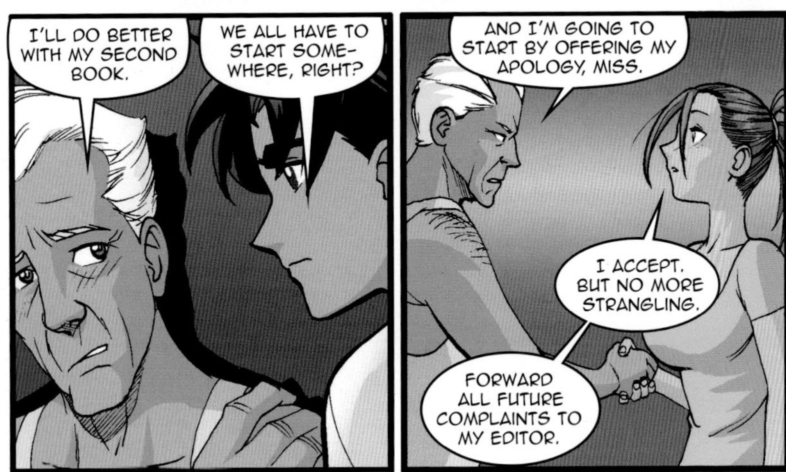
I'LL DO BETTER WITH MY SECOND BOOK.
WE ALL HAVE TO START SOME-WHERE, RIGHT?
AND I'M GOING TO START BY OFFERING MY APOLOGY, MISS.
I ACCEPT. BUT NO MORE STRANGLING.
FORWARD ALL FUTURE COMPLAINTS TO MY EDITOR.

THEY SHOULD CALL THIS TRAIN THE RED HERRING EXPRESS.
EVERY CLUE WE'VE HAD SO FAR POINTS US IN THE WRONG DIRECTION.
NOT EVERY CLUE, JOE.
LET'S SUPPOSE FOR AN INSTANT THAT THE TRAINS DID CRASH AT THE STATION. THERE WOULD HAVE BEEN PRECIOUS LITTLE EVIDENCE TO SIFT THROUGH.
BUT WE WOULD HAVE BEEN AT THE SCENE OF THE CRIME.

AND SOMEONE TRIED TO TIE US IN TO THE INCIDENT WITH THE CONDUCTOR.

WE WERE FRAMED FOR TYING TRE UP IN THE FREEZER, TOO.
HMMM. ARE YOU SAYING...?

THIS ISN'T ABOUT KILLING ANYONE ON THE TRAIN...?
NO. IT'S ABOUT US.
SOMEONE'S TRYING TO FRAME US!

RIGHT THIS MOMENT...
...THAT MIGHT BE THE LEAST OF OUR TROUBLES!
HOW SO, JOE?
IT MIGHT BE MY IMAGINATION, BUT THE TRAIN IS PICKING UP SPEED! FAST!
YOU'RE RIGHT! THE TIME BETWEEN EACH POLE IS GETTING SHORTER!

THE TRAIN IS GOING FASTER BY THE SECOND!

COME ON, WE HAVE TO MOVE QUICKLY.
RIGHT BEHIND YOU!

NO ONE WOULD PUSH THE TRAIN TO THESE LIMITS!
UNLESS THEY WERE TRY-ING TO DERAIL US!

UM, FRANK, WHY ARE WE RACING TO THE REAR OF THE TRAIN?
THE ENGINE IS LOCATED AT THE FRONT!

TRUE, ALONG WITH THE ENGINEER'S CREW. BUT EVERYTHING IS COMPUTERIZED NOW, JOE.
WHICH MEANS A PERSON COULD ACCOMPLISH THE TASK OF HIJACKING THE TRAIN...

...BY HACKING DIRECTLY INTO THE ENGINE'S COMPUTER PROGRAM?
EXACTLY. AND SINCE WE'VE CONCLUDED THAT WE'RE BEING FRAMED...

...WHERE'S THE BEST PLACE TO REPROGRAM THE COMPUTERS FROM?
OUR ROOM!
OR THE REMAINS OF IT, ANYWAY!

INCREDIBLE--THEY'VE HARDWIRED MY COMPUTER RIGHT INTO THE TRAIN'S CIRCUITS!
AS FRAMINGS GO, THESE PEOPLE HAVE THOUGHT OF EVERYTHING.
JOE--THOSE READINGS. THEY'VE OVERRIDDEN THE ACCELERATION SAFEGUARDS!
AND LOCKED THEM INTO PLACE!
THE TRAIN WASN'T DESIGNED TO TRAVEL THIS FAST-- NOT SAFELY!
BUT IF SOMEONE SABOTAGED IT SO WE GO OFF THE RAILS--
--WON'T THAT MEAN THEY'LL BE KILLED ALONG WITH US?!

"NOT NECESSARILY, JOE. NOT IF THEY HAVE AN ESCAPE PLAN!"
IS IT ANY WONDER I ARGUE I MIGHT HAVE THE SMARTEST BROTHER IN THE WORLD?
AND BECAUSE WE'RE GOING WAY TOO FAST FOR SOME-ONE TO SURVIVE A JUMP.
IT MAKES SENSE OUR MYS-TERIOUS ATTACKERS WOULD BE TRYING TO ESCAPE FROM THE ROOF!
CHAPTER NINE:
"RUNAWAY TRAIN!"

BUT HOW? A HANG-GLIDER?
MAYBE A MEETING WITH A HELI-COPTER...EVEN A SMALL PLANE?

WISH I HAD ANOTHER MOMENT TO BRAIN-STORM WITH FRANK...

MAYBE I CAN DISCONNECT IT FROM THE TRAIN'S SYSTEM?
NO. TOO RISKY. IT'S PROBABLY BOOBY-TRAPPED.
I'LL ASK YOU TO HEAD TO THE FRONT OF THE TRAIN ON THE SLIGHT CHANCE YOU CAN OVERRIDE THE CONTROLS FROM THE ENGINE ROOM.

YOU GOING TO BE OKAY HERE?
I'M GOING TO GIVE IT MY BEST SHOT.

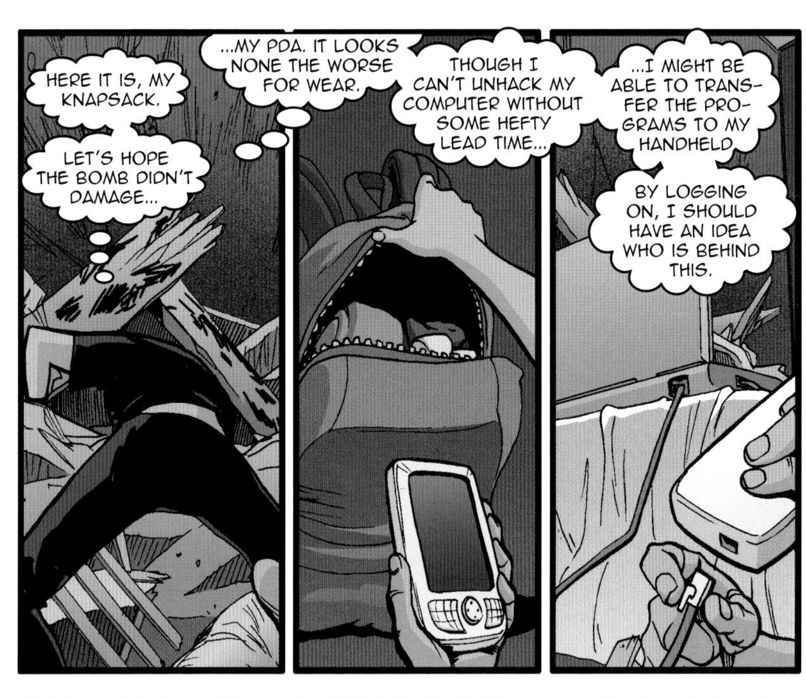
HERE IT IS, MY KNAPSACK.
LET'S HOPE THE BOMB DIDN'T DAMAGE...
...MY PDA. IT LOOKS NONE THE WORSE FOR WEAR.
THOUGH I CAN'T UNHACK MY COMPUTER WITHOUT SOME HEFTY LEAD TIME...
...I MIGHT BE ABLE TO TRANS-FER THE PRO-GRAMS TO MY HANDHELD.
BY LOGGING ON, I SHOULD HAVE AN IDEA WHO IS BEHIND THIS.

WHAT?
WHOEVER IT IS USED PIRATED A.T.A.C. TECHNOLOGY TO DO THIS.
A.T.A.C.

AND I REALIZE NOW WHO HAS BEEN BEHIND IT ALL!

YOU!
NOW IT ALL MAKES SENSE! WHO BETTER TO SET UP THE HARDY BOYS--
--THAN THE NOIR SISTERS?
BUT "SET UP" ISN'T OUR TRUE GOAL. OUR ASSIGNMENT WAS TO SETTLE FOR NOTHING SHORT OF THE DEATH OF YOU AND YOUR BROTHER.
"ASSIGNMENT"?
ARE YOU SAYING YOU WORK FOR A.T.A.C. AS WELL?

NO. WE'VE BEEN BLESSED BY BEING OPERATIVES OF W.A.R.D.
WARRING ADOLESCENTS, REVENGE DIVISION!
IN SHORT, WE'RE AGAINST EVERYTHING A.T.A.C. TRIES TO ACCOM-PLISH.
WE BELIEVE ANARCHY AND CHAOS ARE STRONG-ER FORCES FOR CHANGE THAN JUSTICE.
AND THERE ARE A LOT OF US.
"JUST AS YOUR FATHER PICKED YOU TWO AS HIS FIRST AGENTS...
"...OUR DAD ENTRUSTED US WITH THIS FIRST MISSION.
"AFTER ALL, THE FAMILY THAT SLAYS TOGETHER, STAYS TOGETHER."
OKAY, THAT'S JUST SICK.

NOT TOO JUDGMENTAL, HUH?
UM, YOU'RE THE ONE WHO'S TRYING TO KILL ME.
EMPHASIS ON TRYING!
THERE'S OUR ESCAPE HELICOPTER, JUST LIKE WE ORDERED!
WOK
CHOK

THERE'S NOT ENOUGH ROOM ON THIS SIDE OF THE TUNNEL.
THEY HAVE TO MEET US ON THE OTHER SIDE OF THE MOUNTAIN.
WE'LL BE THERE IN THREE MINUTES--LET'S WRAP IT UP, SHIRA!
HE'S A BETTER MARTIAL ARTIST THAN YOU'D IMAGINE BY LOOKING AT HIM.
NOW WHO'S BEING JUDGMENTAL?
UGHN!

SHIRA!
I CAN APPRECIATE SIBLING CON-CERN, BUT...

IS IT ME, OR IS THE TRAIN... SLOWING?
IT I-IS... BUT...
...HOW IS THAT... POSSIBLE?

DIDN'T YOU GET THE MEMO, NICOLINA?
THIS IS THE AGE OF TECHNOLOGY--ALL THINGS ARE POSSIBLE.
IN THIS CASE, I WAS ABLE TO HACK INTO YOUR HACK OF MY COMPUTER.
ALLOWING ME TO BRING THE SPEEDING TRAIN TO A COMPLETE STOP.

CHAPTER TEN: "THE TUNNEL OF NOT LOVE"

NOT YET!
FWOOOOSH
AAAAH!

THE GIRLS!
BUT THAT BLINDING FLASH OF LIGHT ONLY LASTED FIVE SECONDS!
IT WOULD HAVE BEEN WORSE IF WE WEREN'T WEARING THESE STANDARD ISSUE A.T.A.C. ANTI-MAGNESIUM FLARE LENSES.
EVEN WHEN WE'RE NOT ON OFFICIAL ASSIGNMENT--
IT'S A HANDY GADGET TO HAVE ON HAND.
OR EYE.

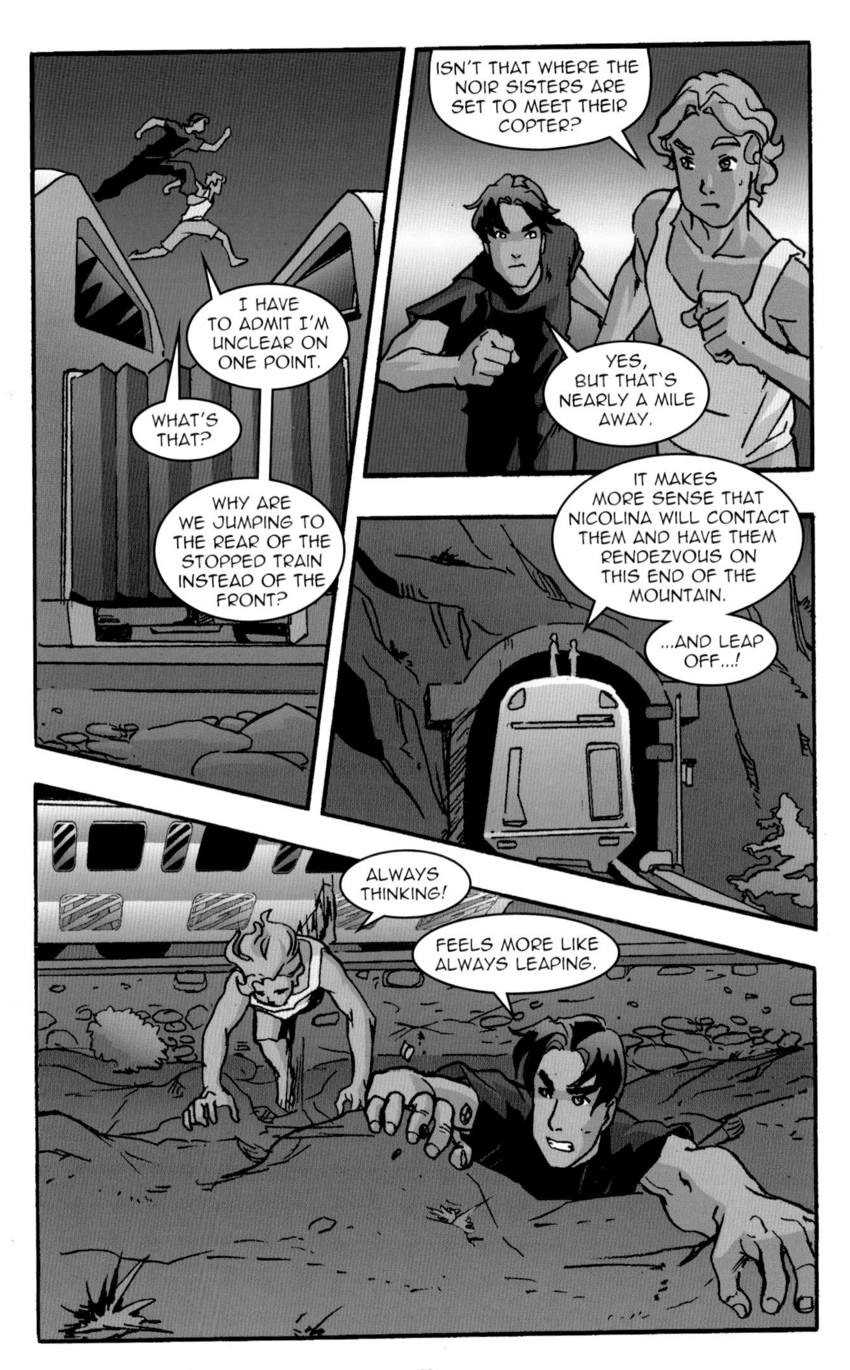
I HAVE TO ADMIT I'M UNCLEAR ON ONE POINT.
WHAT'S THAT?
WHY ARE WE JUMPING TO THE REAR OF THE STOPPED TRAIN INSTEAD OF THE FRONT?
ISN'T THAT WHERE THE NOIR SISTERS ARE SET TO MEET THEIR COPTER?
YES, BUT THAT'S NEARLY A MILE AWAY.
IT MAKES MORE SENSE THAT NICOLINA WILL CONTACT THEM AND HAVE THEM RENDEZVOUS ON THIS END OF THE MOUNTAIN.
...AND LEAP OFF...!
ALWAYS THINKING!
FEELS MORE LIKE ALWAYS LEAPING.

WE MADE IT! NOW ALL WEEEEEEEEEE?!
LADIES.
OOF!
'MEMBER US?
HOW COULD I FOR-GET? I FLIPPED FOR YOU.
NOW IT'S YOUR TURN!
LEAVE MY SISTER ALONE!
IT'S NOT REALLY HER I'M AFTER, SHIRA.
MY GOAL IS TO GRAB THE TRANSMITTER IN HER HAND.
NOT GOING TO HAPPEN, HARDY. MY BACK-UP WILL BE HERE ANY MOMENT!

THAT MIGHT HAVE WORKED OUT PERFECTLY FOR YOU...
IF I HADN'T USED MY PDA TO JAM YOUR TRANSMIT-TER'S SIGNAL.
GRRRR.
LOOKS LIKE IT'S JUST US.
ACTUALLY, THAT'S THE FUNNY THING ABOUT CALLING IN FOR BACK-UP...
IT WORKS BOTH WAYS.
WHO...?
THOSE AREN'T OUR PEOPLE!

WE GOT YOUR EMERGENCY CALL, BOYS.
I PULLED SOME A.T.A.C. STRINGS. FORTUNATELY THERE'S A MARINE BASE NOT FAR FROM HERE.

SOON....
WOW. AS ARCHENEMIES GO, YOU TWO KNOW HOW TO PICK THEM.
WE DIDN'T HAVE MUCH TO DO WITH IT, MR. PENHURST.
YEAH, NIGEL, THEY MAY BE BEAU-TIFUL, BUT THEY'RE ALSO DEADLY.
WE PUT IN THAT CALL TO YOU ONCE WE REALIZED EVERYONE ON BOARD WAS IN DANGER.
SPEAKING OF WHICH...
...WE'VE GOT A TRAIN TO CATCH!
YOU'VE BEEN WANTING TO SAY THAT SINCE WE GOT OUR TICKETS, HAVEN'T YOU?

CHAPTER ELEVEN: "THE END OF THE LINE....?"
FRANK! JOE! HELLO!
CAN I JUST SAY HOW MUCH I LOVE CALIFORNIA ALREADY?
CAN I JUST SAY "DOWN BOY."

MY NAME'S ANGELA, I'M WITH THE *BOARD TO DEATH.*
I'M FRANK AND THIS IS JOE.
THAT'S QUITE THE NAME FOR YOUR COMPETITION.
DON'T LET THE NAME FOOL YOU.
WE TAKE OUR EXTREME SPORTS PRETTY SERIOUSLY AROUND THESE PARTS.
BOARD TO DEATH
BOARD TO DEATH
THAT CERTAINLY SEEMS TO BE THE CASE.
SEND ME IN, COACH.

PLEASE WAIT HERE, I'LL GET THE CAR AND BRING IT AROUND.
IF YOU INSIST.

I DON'T WANT TO DISRUPT YOUR LATEST CASE, BOYS, BUT I THOUGHT YOU SHOULD KNOW.
NIGEL, ARE YOU OKAY?
WHAT HAPPENED?!
THOSE "GIRL-FRIENDS" OF YOURS ARE AS RESOURCEFUL AS YOU TWO ARE.
I'M AFRAID THEY GOT AWAY FROM US.
I DOUBT WE'LL HEAR FROM THEM ANY TIME SOON.
SORRY, GUYS, MY LIMO IS IN THE SHOP.
THIS IS FINE, ANGELA. THANK YOU.

THERE YOU GO.
THANKS, ANGELA.
POP
SO, WHAT DO WE DO ABOUT W.A.R.D. AND THE SISTERS NOIR?
WE KEEP DOING OUR JOB, JOE.
WHICH MEANS WE KEEP PEOPLE LIKE THEM FROM DOING THEIRS.

"BOARD TO DEATH"
CHAPTER ONE:
"A PIRATE HEAD AND A PIRATE HEART!"*
DON'T WORRY, NORA-- YOU'RE SAFE NOW!
YAHHRRRR!
TH-THANK YOU, CAPTAIN FRANK...BUT I D-DON'T FEEL VERY SAFE YET.
*APOLOGIES TO GILBERT AND SULLIVAN.

COME HAVE A TASTE OF WOOD, YE SCABBY DOGS!
'TIS THE VERY LEAST YE DESERVE FOR KIDNAPPING THE VICE PRESIDENT'S WEE WAIF OF A DAUGHTER!
WHILE ON VACATION, NO LESS!
WE'RE GOING TO GET AWAY WITH IT TOO, PUNK!
AND STOP TALKING LIKE THAT, IT IS ANNOYING!

YOU'LL BE BACK WITH YOUR MOM AND DAD BEFORE YOU KNOW IT. TRUST US!

HOW ABOUT A SWAT TO YE HEAD?
WHAP
UGNH!
DOES THAT BE ANNOYING AS WELL?
SPLASH
SOMETIMES YOU DON'T WIN BY FIGHTING.
WHO ARE YOU FIGHTING, CAPTAIN FRANK?
THE PIRATES ARE BEHIND US.

TAP TAP
I'M LOOKING FOR SOMETHING.
AHOY--
-- I'VE FOUND IT! JUST AS I SUSPECTED!
I DON'T UNDERSTAND.
HOW CAN YOU TOUCH THE SKY?
BECAUSE IT ISN'T A SKY AT ALL!
IT IS A WALL PAINTED TO LOOK LIKE A SKY!
FLICK
AND THERE'S A DOOR, JUST WHERE I THOUGHT IT WOULD BE!
YOU'RE SMART!
FOR A PIRATE... HA HA!

HOLD ON TIGHT!
WEEEE!
SPROING
JOE, COME ON! WE RESCUED THE GIRL--WE NEED TO GET WHILE THE GETTING'S GOOD!
COUNT YESELVES LUCKY, YE LAND LUBBERS!
THUMP
BY THE GRACE OF THE SEVEN SEAS--
--YE'LL LIVE TO FIGHT ANOTHER DAY!
YOU'RE ENJOYING THIS PIRATE THING A LITTLE TOO MUCH, JOE.

WHUMP
THBUMP
THAT SHOULD HOLD THEM FOR A MOMENT!
THANK YOU, PIRATE JOE...YOU AND YOUR BROTHER ARE SO BRAVE!
IT WAS OUR PLEASURE, NORA.
YOU'RE THE CUTEST PIRATE EVER!
AWWW.
WE NEED TO KEEP MOVING, KIDS.
WE'RE NOT OUT OF DANGER UNTIL WE'RE OUT OF THIS BUILDING.

WE SHOULD BE ABLE TO GET HER OUT SAFELY IF WE STORM IN FROM THE MAIN ENTRANCE.
YOU'LL DO NO SUCH THING. I'LL NOT RISK MY DAUGHTER BEING HARMED!
YES, SIR, MR. VICE PRESIDENT.

SIR, WE JUST GOT WORD FROM A.T.A.C.*--
--THEY HAD THE HARDY BOYS WORKING UNDERCOVER ON THE RIDE, JUST IN CASE.
THE BEST NEWS I'VE HEARD ALL MORNING.
*A.T.A.C.-- AMERICAN TEENS AGAINST CRIME!

NORA! YOU'RE SAFE!
MOMMY!
HOLD YOUR FIRE, OFFICERS!
THEY'RE THE GOOD GUYS.
MOVE! MOVE! MOVE!
SECURE THE BUILDING, NOW!
I OWE YOU TWO MY GRATITUDE!
ALL IN A DAY'S WORK FOR A PIRATE, SIR.
PIRATE JOE AND HIS BROTHER ARE FUN!
YARRH.

SOON...
I CAN'T BELIEVE YOU SAID "YARH" TO THE VICE PRESIDENT.
HE LAUGHED.

YOU DID A GREAT JOB TODAY, BOYS.
I TRUST YOU'RE READY FOR YOUR NEXT ASSIGN-MENT?
THAT VOICE--IT'S THE SAME ONE ON OUR ASSIGNMENT CARTRIDGES.
IT CAN ONLY BE ONE PER-SON--
--NIGHT OWL PENTHOUSE!

DON'T BOTHER TRYING TO MAKE ME LAUGH, JOE.
YOU KNOW VERY WELL MY NAME IS NIGEL PENHURST.
YOUR FATHER WAS RIGHT TO ENLIST YOU TWO AS A.T.A.C.'S FIRST UNDERCOVER TEENS.

THERE ARE A LOT OF TEENS IN TROUBLE THE COUNTRY OVER.
NOT ONLY DO BOYS SUCH AS YOU SERVE AS ROLE MODELS, YOU RISK YOUR LIVES TO KEEP PEOPLE SAFE.
I DOUBT THAT I WAS AS BRAVE AS YOU TWO WHEN I WAS YOUR AGE.
THAT'S KIND OF YOU TO SAY, SIR. IT'S AN HONOR FOR US TO BE A PART OF A.T.A.C.
SPEAKING OF WHICH, AREN'T WE HERE IN LOS ANGELES FOR A SPECIFIC CASE?
THAT'S EXACTLY RIGHT, JOE...

LATER...
CHAPTER TWO: "DANGER ON TWO WHEELS"
JOE, FRANK-- IT'S SO EXCITING TO SEE YOU HERE!
IT'S A PLEASURE, ANGELA. YOU'VE REALLY DONE A GREAT JOB OF ORGANIZING THIS EVENT.

THAT'S PUTTING IT MILDLY. I'VE SEEN THE BROCHURES, SURE, AND THE WEBSITE --
--BUT SEEING IT LIVE?

AXF
LOOPS, WAVES, TUNNELS, JUMPS-- THIS PLACE HAS IT ALL.

WHEN YOU PEOPLE SAY "EXTREME" YOU MEAN IT!
THAT IS ONE INTIMIDATING SKATEBOARD COURSE.
WE TRY TO LIVE UP TO OUR NAME.

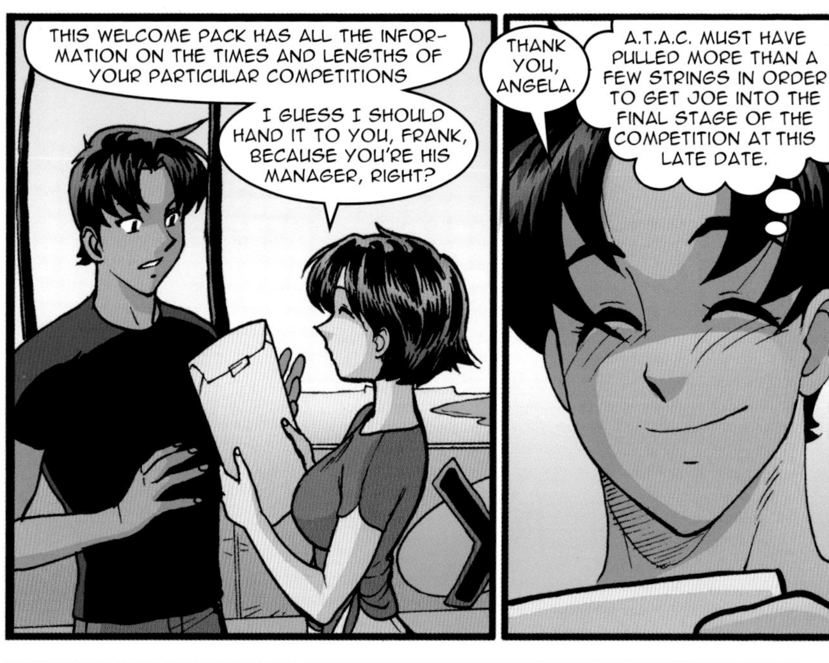
THIS WELCOME PACK HAS ALL THE INFORMATION ON THE TIMES AND LENGTHS OF YOUR PARTICULAR COMPETITIONS
I GUESS I SHOULD HAND IT TO YOU, FRANK, BECAUSE YOU'RE HIS MANAGER, RIGHT?
THANK YOU, ANGELA.
A.T.A.C. MUST HAVE PULLED MORE THAN A FEW STRINGS IN ORDER TO GET JOE INTO THE FINAL STAGE OF THE COMPETITION AT THIS LATE DATE.

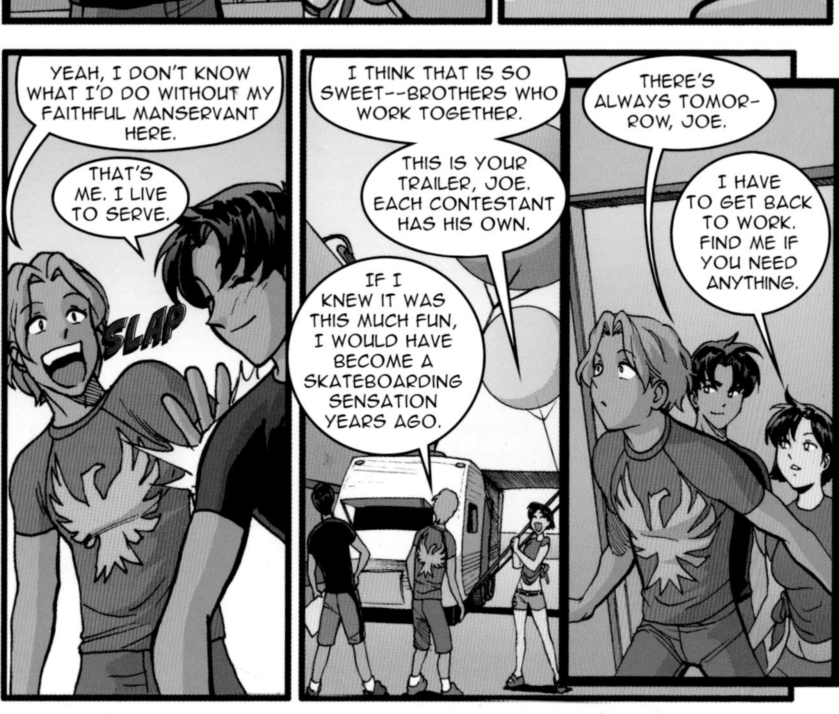
YEAH, I DON'T KNOW WHAT I'D DO WITHOUT MY FAITHFUL MANSERVANT HERE.
THAT'S ME. I LIVE TO SERVE.
SLAP
I THINK THAT IS SO SWEET--BROTHERS WHO WORK TOGETHER.
THIS IS YOUR TRAILER, JOE. EACH CONTESTANT HAS HIS OWN.
IF I KNEW IT WAS THIS MUCH FUN, I WOULD HAVE BECOME A SKATEBOARDING SENSATION YEARS AGO.
THERE'S ALWAYS TOMORROW, JOE.
I HAVE TO GET BACK TO WORK. FIND ME IF YOU NEED ANYTHING.

I HOPE YOU'RE NOT UPSET THAT A.T.A.C. PLACED ME IN THE COMPETITION INSTEAD OF YOU. I'M SURE IT'S ONLY BECAUSE I'M YOUNGER.
NOT A PROBLEM, JOE...

...THEY DIDN'T WANT TO PUT IN ANYONE THAT WOULD THROW OFF THE COMPETITION BY ACTUALLY WINNING.
HEY--

--THAT IS ONE AWE-SOME BOARD! THAT NIGEL THINKS OF EVERYTHING!
EVERYTHING BUT THE ACTUAL GAME CARTRIDGE WITH OUR CASE IN IT.
IT SHOULD BE HERE SOME-WHERE.

KNOCK, KNOCK
IT'S ANGELA.
HAS THE CONTEST STARTED ALREADY?

WHOOPS. I ALMOST FORGOT.
THIS WAS LEFT FOR YOU AT THE FRONT GATE.
OH, RIGHT. THANKS. WE WERE EXPECT-ING THIS.
GOOD THING A.T.A.C. HAS FIGURED OUT HOW TO ADAPT THESE ASSIGNMENT CARTRIDGES TO MULTI-PLATFORMS.
IT CERTAINLY GIVES US MOR OPTIONS IN LEAR THE SPECIFICS AB EACH CASE.

HELLO, HARDY BOYS.
AS YOU KNOW, NATIONAL EXTREME SPORTS EVENTS ARE VERY COMPETITIVE.
A.T.A.C.
THERE IS A LOT OF PRIZE MONEY AND CORPORATE SPONSORSHIPS AT STAKE.
OVER THE PAST SEVERAL MONTHS, ALL ACROSS THE COUNTRY--
--SOMEONE HAS MADE CERTAIN SOME WOULD-BE CONTESTANTS WOULD NEVER MAKE IT TO THE FINALS.
YOUR ASSIGNMENT HERE IS TWO-FOLD:
PROTECT THE TEENS HERE AT THE GAMES--
--AND FIND THE PERSON RESPONSIBLE.
WHAT ABOUT WINNING? SHOULDN'T I--?
SHUSH.

LIKE ALL YOUNG PARTICIPANTS, DEXTER THOMAS USES A NICKNAME WHILE BOARDING.
DEX THOM HANDLES THE BOARD LIKE A MASTER VIOLINIST DOES THE BOW.
THAT'S QUITE A GROUP, HUNH?
ECLECTIC TO SAY THE LEAST.
I WONDER IF--OH.
HEY, I WAS JUST POPPING OVER TO SAY "WELCOME!"
SO, WELCOME!
THANK YOU. I'M JOE HARDY AND THIS IS FRANK.
"JOE"? I'M DEX THOM.
AND MAY THE BEST MAN WIN.
I'LL SEE YOU AT THE LUNCH AREA, GUYS? I'M STARVING.
WE'LL BE RIGHT OVER.
WELL, THAT WAS CERTAINLY POLITE.
NOT WHAT YOU'D EXPECT FROM A COMPETITION WITH "EXTREME" IN THE TITLE.

THIS DARING YOUNG LADY GOES ONLY BY THE NAME OF PINKSHADE.
EVEN WE HAVE BEEN UNABLE TO LEARN HER REAL NAME.

DON'T LET THE "NICE GUY" ROUTINE FOOL YOU-- DEX IS A SHARK.
I'M PINKSHADE.
IF YOU FORGET, JUST CALL ME "WINNER."

PINKSHADE. PRACTICE IS IN ORDER.
YOU'RE RIGHT, OF COURSE.

LATER... LOSER.
UM...

MR. KAO MOTO IS A MASTER TRAINER FROM ASIA.
OLD SCHOOL.
SHE'S A STRANGE BIRD, THAT ONE.
I'M THINKING COO-COO.
I AM HER TRAINER, MR. MOTO. I APOLOGIZE FOR HER RUDENESS.
ACTUALLY, IT WAS KIND OF HOT.

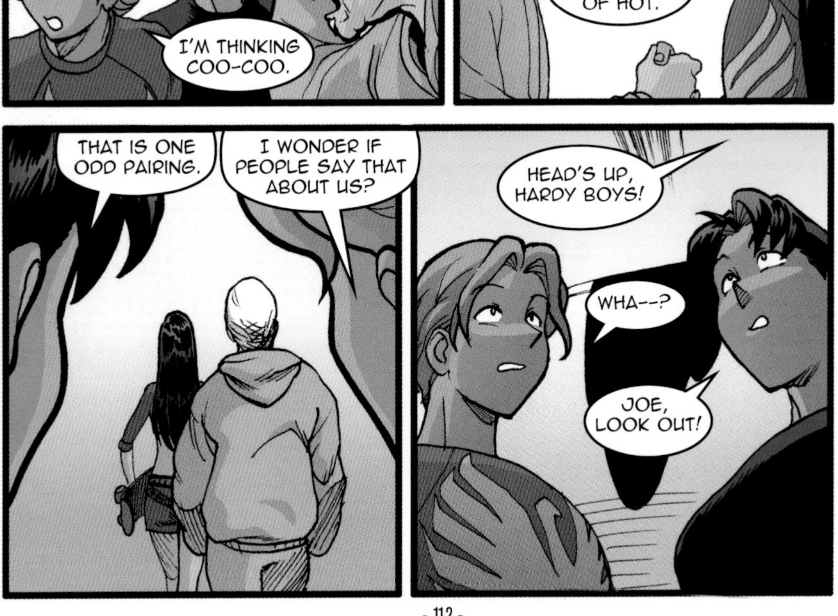
THAT IS ONE ODD PAIRING.
I WONDER IF PEOPLE SAY THAT ABOUT US?
HEAD'S UP, HARDY BOYS!
WHA--?
JOE, LOOK OUT!

TED LAUBER GOES BY THE MONIKER... THE WRAITH.
FOR OBVIOUS REASONS.

FWOSH

HI, I'M--

WHAT A CHARACTER, HUH?
QUITE THE CAST OF ODDBALLS.

A PURIST WHO SKATES FOR THE SAKE OF THE SPORT--
--SAM ROBERTS RELUCTANTLY TOOK THE NAME "COURAGE."
IT WASN'T ALWAYS THIS WAY. IN THE OLD DAYS, PEOPLE JUST SKATED FOR THE LOVE OF THE SPORT.
IN RECENT YEARS IT'S BECOME SHOW BUSINESS.
APPARENTLY.
NO ONE WILL ACCUSE YOU OF HAVING STYLE.

WHAT IS THAT SUPPOSED TO--
POK
JUST KIDDING YOU, KID.

"KID" IS RIGHT. HE'S ALMOST TOO OLD FOR THIS CONTEST.
TRUE. BUT HE DID HAVE A POINT...

SOON...
...AT A SECOND HAND SHOP NEAR THE VENICE BOARDWALK...

EXPLAIN THIS TO ME AGAIN, FRANK?
IT'S SIMPLE, JOE. WHEN IN ROME, DRESS LIKE ROMANS.
IF EVERY-ONE IN THE GAME HAS A STAGE PER-SONA, YOU NEED ONE TOO.
IT FEELS... IMPURE.
WE ARE UNDERCOVER, JOE.

LOOK WHAT I FOUND IN THE ANTIQUE SECTION.
WOW, HOW ARE YOU LIFTING IT?
IT'S FOAM RUBBER, SILLY. SEE?

BOP
USE YOUR HEAD.
HEH HEH.

HERE YOU GO, JOE.
"JOE?"
WHO IS THIS "JOE" OF WHOM YOU SPEAK?

THE YOUNG MAN YOU CALLED JOE HARDY IS NO MORE!
NOW AND FOREVERMORE, I AM--
--HARDCASE!
NOW YOU'RE GETTING INTO THE SPIRIT.
BRAVO!
LET ALL WHO OPPOSE ME... FEAR ME!
CLAP CLAP CLAP CLAP
BRRRR
I'M FEARING.
THIS IS SILLY. I'M GOING TO CHANGE.
YOU LOOK GREAT.
WE HAVE TO GO NOW OR YOU'LL BE LATE.

THAT CROWD... ARE THEY ALL HERE TO SEE US?
ME, ANY WAY.
THAT'S ONE HEALTHY EGO YOU HAVE THERE, DEX.
YOU SHOULD ALL BE WORRYING ABOUT GETTING IN A PRACTICE.
WE WILL-- ONCE PINKSHADE COMPLETES HER RUN.
SHE NEEDS THE SPACE TO CON-CENTRATE.
THAT'S ONE BRAVE GIRL.
I AGREE.
HMM.
ALMOST FEEL BAD SHE'S GOING TO LOSE.
YOU ALL ARE.
UH OH.
THIS CAN'T BE RIGHT...!

MR. MOTO--
YOU HAVE TO
STOP HER!
GOOD
LUCK WITH
THAT. SHE'S
GOT A MIND OF
HER OWN,
THAT ONE.

BUT LOOK! THE
RAMP ENDS NOT
IN A JUMP--
--BUT FLAT
INTO THAT
WALL!
IT
SHOULDN'T
BE THERE!
SHE'LL BE
KILLED!

STOP!
NO!
PINKSHADE,
DON'T!
WAIT!
WAIT!
DON'T
GO!
PINKSHADE!
CAN'T HEAR
THEM FROM UP
HERE.

THEY MUST BE
GIVING ME THE ALL
CLEAR!

SHOWTIME.

CHAPTER THREE:
"CAUGHT FLAT-
FOOTED"
NOOOOOO!
FRANK--?!
COME ON, WE'VE ONLY GOT SECONDS TO SPARE!

BEHIND THE TRACK?
WHAT CAN WE DO BACK HERE?
THAT'S THE REAR OF THE WALL SHE'S GOING TO HIT!
AND IT'S ONLY BEING HELD UP BY THOSE 2X4s!
OH, NO! THAT WALL SHOULDN'T BE THERE!
NO TIME TO STOP!
SLAM
PRAY THIS WORKS!

UMPH!
WOLFPH!
IS SHE OKAY?
FINGERS CROSSED.

I DON'T KNOW HOW YOU DID IT...
... BUT THANKS!
NOT A PROBLEM.
HOW'D WE PULL THAT ONE OFF?

IF ANYTHING HAS HAPPENED TO HER...
LET'S THINK POSITIVE.
THERE SHE IS!

FORTUNATELY, THESE BALES OF HAY HELPED ME COME TO A STOP BEFORE I HIT THE PARKING LOT.
I'M WINDED, BUT OKAY.

DON'T MOVE YET, PINKSHADE.
LET'S MAKE SURE THERE ARE NO BROKEN BONES.
YOUR SAFETY IS MORE IMPORTANT THAN THIS CONTEST.

I CONCUR. PERHAPS WE SHOULD POSTPONE ALL OF THIS UNTIL WE CAN ASSURE EVERYONE'S SAFETY?

NO WAY! I DIDN'T JUST RISK MY LIFE FOR NO REASON!
I INTEND TO WIN, NO MATTER HOW MANY PEOPLE TRY TO KILL ME!
MAYBE ANGELA IS RIGHT. WE CAN ALWAYS--

NONE OF US TRAVELED ALL THIS WAY TO GIVE UP.
THAT'S THE SPIRIT.

THIS ISN'T THE ONLY COM-PETITION THAT'S GONE AWRY.
WE KNEW WHAT THE CHANCES WERE GOING INTO THIS.

WELL, UNTIL IT STARTS--
--I WANT YOU SAFE AND SOUND IN YOUR TRAILER!
BUT, MR. MOTO...
IT MIGHT BE BETTER IF WE ALL STAYED TOGETHER, SIR.
SAFETY IN NUMBERS AND ALL THAT.
PLEASE, REST ASSURED WE'RE DOING EVERYTHING WE CAN.
WE DON'T EXPECT ANY FURTHER INCIDENTS.

IT'S THE UNEXPECTED YOU HAVE TO WORRY ABOUT.

THIS IS TURNING INTO A DISASTER.
IF ANYONE GETS HURT, I AM GOING TO FEEL TERRIBLE.

WE'LL FIND THE PERSON OR PERSONS RESPONSIBLE FOR THIS, ANGELA.
YOU HAVE A CONTEST TO RUN.

THANK YOU, FRANK. THE POINT OF THIS THING IS TO HAVE FUN.
WE NEVER THOUGHT WE'D HAVE TO HIRE SECURITY.

A.T.A.C. WAS RIGHT AGAIN. THESE KIDS ARE AT RISK HERE.
IT DOESN'T MAKE SENSE. WHO WOULD WANT TO HURT THEM...?
...OTHER THAN OTHER... COMPETITORS?
I SEE YOUR POINT.

WRAITH--THAT'S COURAGE'S BOARD YOUR HOLDING IN YOUR HAND
I KNOW THAT, HARDY.
AND I KNOW HOW THIS LOOKS.
HERE, I DON'T WANT TO HAVE ANYTHING TO DO WITH IT.
I JUST FOUND IT HERE BEHIND THE TRAILERS.
I WAS GOING TO RETURN IT TO COURAGE WHEN YOU TWO FOUND ME.

LIAR!
DO YOU THINK I'M STUPID?!
POW
HEY!
THERE'S NO CAUSE FOR THAT, COURAGE.
HE MIGHT BE TELLING THE TRUTH.
THE TRUTH IS... I DON'T NEED TO CHEAT TO BEAT YOU.

YEAH.
GOOD LUCK WITH THAT!

IF IT MEANS ANYTHING, I FOUND IT DISCARDED OVER HERE.

WHATEVER. I GOT A CONTEST TO WIN!
DON'T TAKE IT PERSONALLY, WRAITH. EVERYONE IS A LITTLE TENSE.

SAVE IT FOR THE LOSER'S CIRCLE, HARDCASE.

SKATEBOARDERS AREN'T THE HAPPIEST PEOPLE IN THE WORLD.
NOT COMPETITIVE SKATEBOARDERS ANYWAY.

SOON...
LADIES AND GENTLEMAN, LET'S GIVE IT UP FOR--
SK8
--COURAGE!
LET THE GAMES BEGIN!
YEEEAAAHH!
HE'S GOT QUITE THE GAME FACE, I'LL GIVE HIM THAT.
HE CERTAINLY LOOKS LIKE HE'S HAVING FUN.

THAT'S THE WHOLE PROBLEM RIGHT THERE, ISN'T IT?

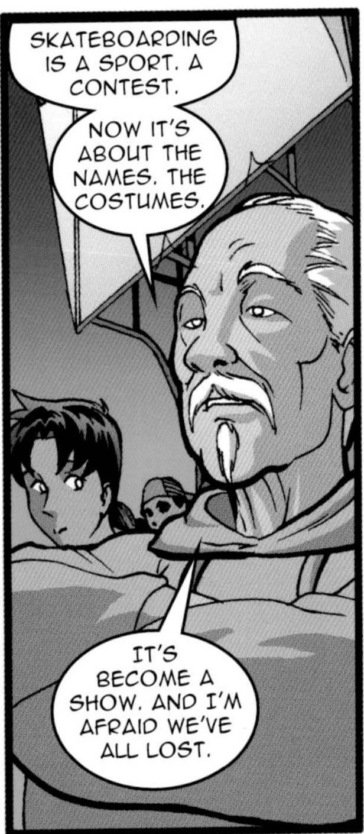
SKATEBOARDING IS A SPORT. A CONTEST.
NOW IT'S ABOUT THE NAMES. THE COSTUMES.
IT'S BECOME A SHOW. AND I'M AFRAID WE'VE ALL LOST.

LOOK!
SOMETHING'S WRONG!

WHAT THE--?!
WOBBLE WOBBLE

JOE, THERE'S THE PROBLEM...!

"... HIS WHEELS! THEY'RE COMING OFF!"

ULP!
GOING TOO FAST...CAN'T STOP...!
WOBBLE

CHAPTER FOUR:
"THEY DIE THROUGH THE AIR WITH THE GREATEST OF EASE...!"
THIS IS GOING TO HURT.
LOTS.
POING

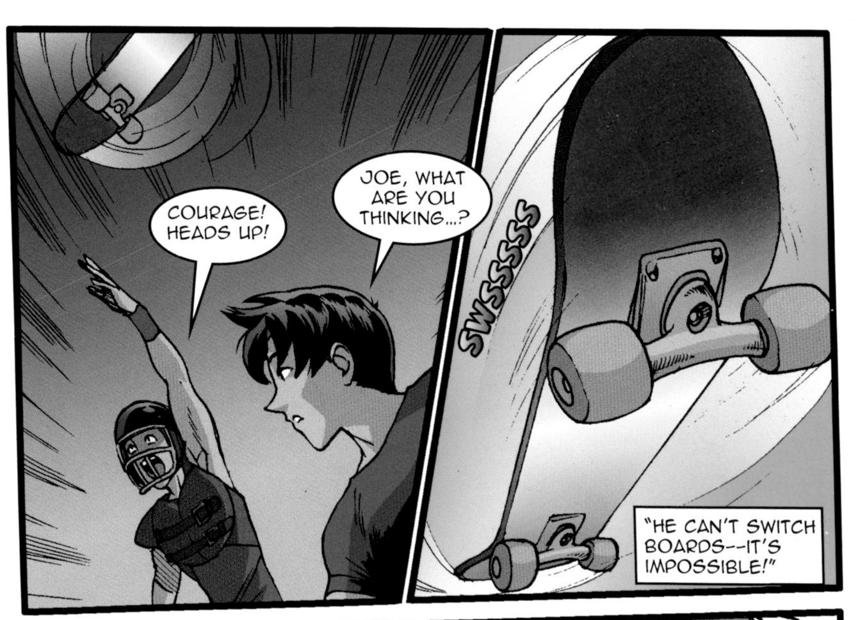
COURAGE! HEADS UP!
JOE, WHAT ARE YOU THINKING...?
SWSSSSSS
"HE CAN'T SWITCH BOARDS--IT'S IMPOSSIBLE!"

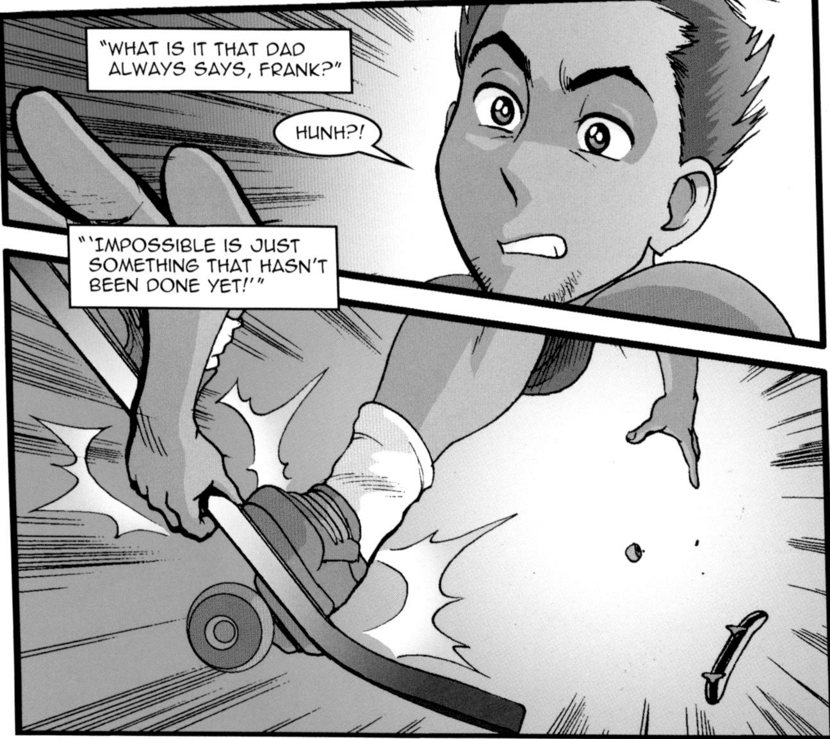
"WHAT IS IT THAT DAD ALWAYS SAYS, FRANK?"
HUNH?!
"'IMPOSSIBLE IS JUST SOMETHING THAT HASN'T BEEN DONE YET!'"

WHOA!
THWAK

HE DID IT!
A PERFECT LANDING!
YEAH!
I'VE NEVER SEEN ANYTHING LIKE IT!
AMAZING!
ARE YOU ALL RIGHT?
I'LL BE FINE--BUT MY BOARD IS GONNA NEED SOME WORK!

AS MUCH AS IT PAINS ME TO SAY THIS TO THE COMPETITION--
THANKS FOR THE SAVE.
I'M SURE YOU'D DO THE SAME FOR ME.
I KNOW WHAT I'M GOING TO DO TO THIS FREAK WHO TRIED TO KILL ME!
ARE YOU ACCUSING ME OF-- ?
EVERYONE SAW YOU MESSING WITH MY BOARD, JERK!
MESSING?! I TOLD YOU, I FOUND--
GUYS!
LIAR! YOU'RE GOING DOWN!
AND YOU CAN GO TO--
POW
THIS ISN'T HELPING ANYTHING!

IT'S HELPING ME--
--I FEEL BETTER ALREADY!
KICK
URPHN!
WE ALL WANT PEOPLE TO TREAT SKATEBOARDING AS A RESPECTABLE SPORT--
--BUT THAT MEANS WE HAVE TO SHOW SOME SPORTS-MANSHIP.
HARDCASE IS RIGHT. LET'S TALK THIS THROUGH.

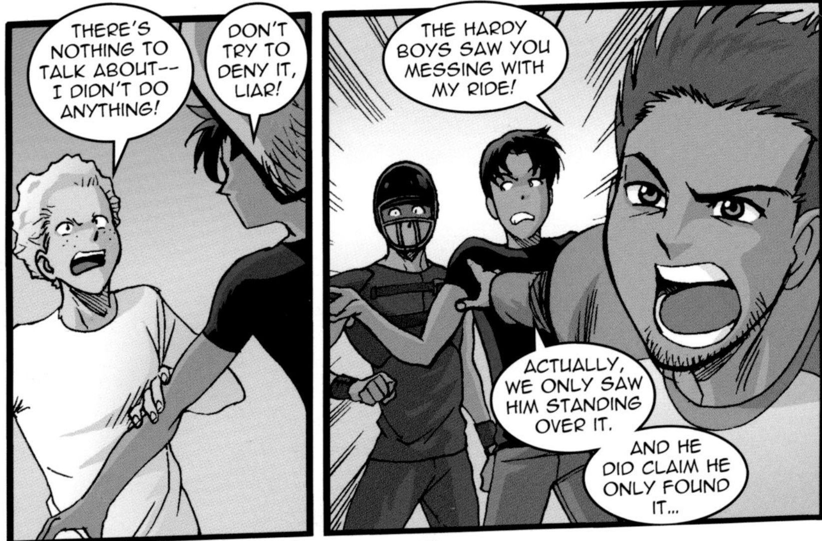
THERE'S NOTHING TO TALK ABOUT-- I DIDN'T DO ANYTHING!
DON'T TRY TO DENY IT, LIAR!
THE HARDY BOYS SAW YOU MESSING WITH MY RIDE!
ACTUALLY, WE ONLY SAW HIM STANDING OVER IT.
AND HE DID CLAIM HE ONLY FOUND IT...

NOW WHAT?!
THIS WHITE-HAIRED FREAK TRIED TO KILL ME!
NO, I DIDN'T!
YOU'RE BOTH LUCKY I DON'T DISQUALIFY YOU FOR FIGHTING!
BUT SINCE WE'RE ALL UNDER A LOT OF STRESS, I'LL LET IT GO THIS TIME.
MORE THAN FAIR.

IF YOU CAN'T KEEP THE CONTESTANTS SAFE--
--THIS WHOLE COMPETITION SHOULD BE SHUT DOWN!

THIS GUY STOLE MY BOARD AND--
ENOUGH! WRAITH?
I WAS CONCERNED ABOUT PINK-SHADE...

...SO I WAS HEADED OVER TO HER TRAILER TO CHECK UP ON HER.

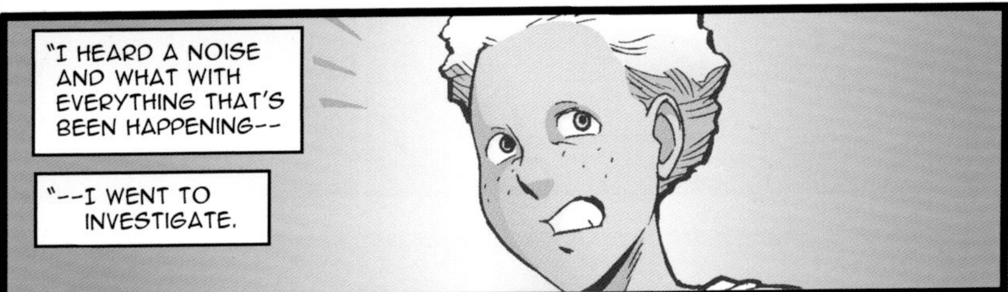
"I HEARD A NOISE AND WHAT WITH EVERYTHING THAT'S BEEN HAPPENING--
"--I WENT TO INVESTIGATE.

"THERE IT WAS AND SOMEONE RACING OFF.
"I'M SORRY I COULDN'T SEE WHO IT WAS."

AND THAT'S WHERE WE CAME IN.
I'M THE BEST ONE IN THE CONTEST--THE LAST THING I NEED TO DO IS KILL THE COMPETITION.
IT'S AN ODDLY COMPELLING ARGUMENT.

THERE DOESN'T SEEM TO BE ENOUGH EVIDENCE TO ACCUSE WRAITH OF BEING ANYTHING OTHER THAN--
--BEING IN THE WRONG PLACE AT THE WRONG TIME.

FINE! I'LL KICK HIS BUTT THE EASY WAY--
--BY WINNING!

I HOPE I MADE THE RIGHT DECISION.
HE DESERVES THE BENEFIT OF THE DOUBT.
FOR NOW.

I JUST HOPE NOTHING HAPPENS TO DEX--
--OR I'LL GET BLAMED FOR THAT TOO.

HE'S GOING TO TRY TO RIDE HIS BOARD ALL THE WAY DOWN THE RAILING?
I'M GLAD I'M NOT DOING THAT ONE!

IF THIS DOESN'T PUT ME OVER THE TOP... NOTHING WILL!

CHAPTER FIVE:
"BOARD INTO SUBMISSION!"
HA! THE CROWD IS GOING WILD!
NOT THAT I BLAME THEM-- THEY RECOGNIZE GREATNESS WHEN THEY SEE IT!

HE CERTAINLY KNOWS HOW TO PUT ON A SHOW.
HE'S AWESOME--I'LL GIVE HIM THAT.
AND I'LL GIVE THE CROWD A ONCE OVER. OUR KILLER COULD BE...

"...ANYWHERE!
"THERE--ON THE ROOFTOP! IT'S THE BARREL OF A RIFLE!
"AND I'M BETTING ITS AIMED AT DEX!"

JOE! ROOFTOP! CAREFUL! NOW!
I SEE IT, FRANK--I'M ON IT!

I HOPE I'M REMEMBERING THIS CORRECTLY.
IF I'M RIGHT, IT SHOULD BE RIGHT ABOUT HERE...

YES! THE FUSE BOX!
JUDGING FROM ITS SIZE, IT CONTROLS THE LIGHTS FOR THE WHOLE STADIUM!

OUR SNIPER CAN'T SHOOT DEX--
FLIP
--IF HE CAN'T SEE DEX!

WHAT THE--?!
WHO TURNED OUT THE LIGHTS?!

PING PING
WHAT THE--?! IT'S PITCH BLACK!
AND SOMEONE'S SHOOTING AT ME?
MAN, THIS IS ONE COMPETITIVE CONTEST!

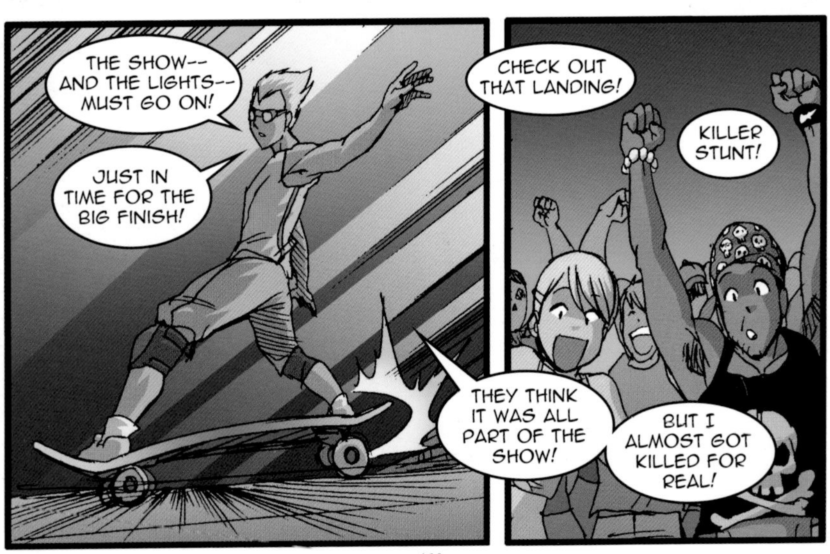
THE SHOW-- AND THE LIGHTS-- MUST GO ON!
JUST IN TIME FOR THE BIG FINISH!
CHECK OUT THAT LANDING!
KILLER STUNT!
THEY THINK IT WAS ALL PART OF THE SHOW!
BUT I ALMOST GOT KILLED FOR REAL!

YOU ROCK!
THAT WAS YOUR BEST RIDE YET!
WHO AM I TO ARGUE WITH MY FANS?
FRANK, WHAT'S HAPPENING?
WERE THOSE BULLETS THAT NEARLY HIT DEX?!
YES! JOE WENT UP THERE TO INVESTIGATE.
I'VE GOT TO HURRY! HE MAY NEED MY HELP!

THAT FRANK IS ONE BRAVE DUDE!
I'VE NEVER SEEN AN ASSISTANT WORK SO HARD!

I HEARD THOSE GUNSHOTS OVER THE ROAR OF THE FANS.
I HAVE TO BE READY FOR ANYTHING. THE SNIPER COULD STILL BE HERE.
CRASH
OR HE COULD BE GONE.
LUCKILY HE WAS IN SUCH A HURRY--
--HE LEFT BEHIND HIS GUN.

WE NEED TO GET THE RIFLE TO A LAB RIGHT AWAY-- TO CHECK FOR PRINTS.
THANKS TO THE TECH GUYS AT A.T.A.C., WE DON'T HAVE TO WAIT.
I COMPLETELY FORGOT YOU HAD THAT DEVICE.
IT'S BECAUSE THEY MAKE THESE HIGH TECH GADGETS LOOK SO NORMAL.
OTHERWISE EVERYONE WILL WANT ONE!
THIS THERMO-MAGNETICALLY TREATED LENS SHOULD INSTANTLY BE ABLE TO CAPTURE ANY FINGERPRINTS.
RIGHT, AND TRANSMIT THEM TO A.T.A.C. FOR INSTANT IDENTIFICATION.

ANYTHING?
NADA. CLEAN AS A WHISTLE.

YOU BOYS SHOULDN'T BE UP HERE.
WE GOT A REPORT OF SHOTS FIRED--YOU COULD BE IN DANGER.
THANKS FOR YOUR CONCERN, OFFICERS.

WE'RE STILL NO CLOSER TO STOPPING THIS GUY.
MAYBE IT'S NOT A GUY WE'RE LOOKING FOR AT ALL.
ONE OF THE CONTESTANTS HAS NO ALIBI DURING THE SHOOTING.
PINKSHADE HAS SUPPOSEDLY BEEN IN HER TRAILER THIS WHOLE TIME.

THERE'S NOTHING TO SAY SHE COULDN'T BE OUR SHOOTER.
HARDLY IRONCLAD, BUT WE SHOULD AT LEAST CHECK IT OUT.

I DON'T KNOW, FRANK. WE'VE BEEN AT THIS LONG ENOUGH TO KNOW--
--THAT THERE ARE A LOT OF REASONS WHY A PERSON WILL DO SOMETHING TERRIBLE, BUT--
BUT MURDER OVER A SKATE-BOARDING TITLE?
I ADMIT IT BOGGLES THE MIND.

HOLD UP, YOU TWO!
HOW DO WE KNOW YOU TWO AREN'T THE ONES WHO TRIED TO MURDER THE OTHERS?
MAYBE BECAUSE WE KEEP RESCUING EVERY-ONE?

KNOCK KNOCK
PINKSHADE? ARE YOU THERE?
HMM.
GOOD POINT.

Y-YES! YES, I'M HERE!
BUT I'M TRAPPED--I'VE BEEN LOCKED INSIDE!

WE'LL HAVE YOU OUT IN A MOMENT!
STAND BACK!
KRACK
THANK YOU SO MUCH! I WAS AFRAID I WAS GOING TO MISS THE COM-PETITION!
ARE YOU OKAY, SWEETIE?!
I AM NOW, HONEY!
THEY'RE... GOING OUT?
HOW'D WE MISS THAT CLUE?
WE WEREN'T LOOKING.
I THINK IT'S SWEET.

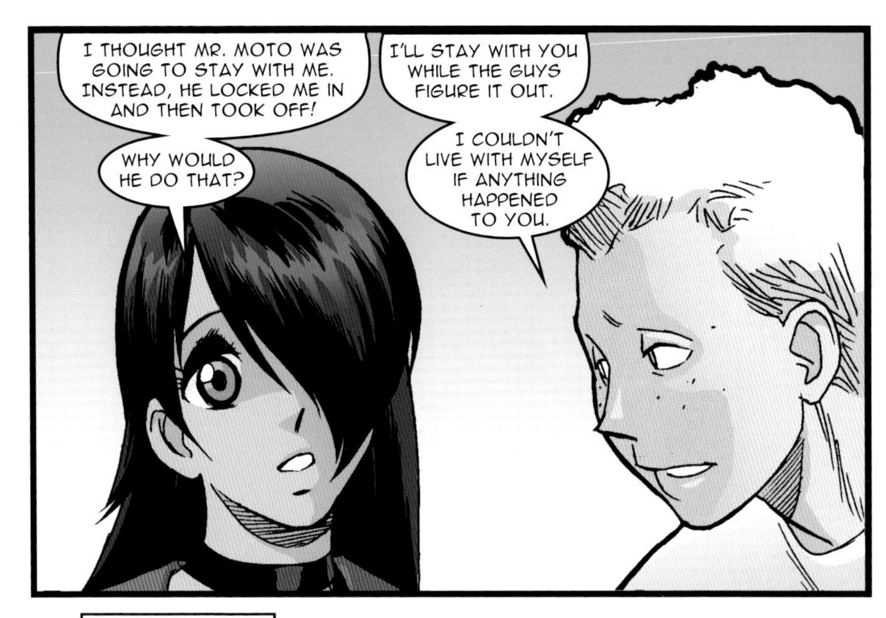
I THOUGHT MR. MOTO WAS GOING TO STAY WITH ME. INSTEAD, HE LOCKED ME IN AND THEN TOOK OFF!
WHY WOULD HE DO THAT?
I'LL STAY WITH YOU WHILE THE GUYS FIGURE IT OUT.
I COULDN'T LIVE WITH MYSELF IF ANYTHING HAPPENED TO YOU.

MOMENTS LATER, AT THE LOUNGE...
WE'VE TRIED EVERYWHERE ELSE HERE AT THE SHOW.
IF IT IS MR. MOTO, I HOPE WE FIND HIM BEFORE HE HURTS SOMEONE.

UH OH.
I HATE TO SOUND SO GLIB--

CHAPTER SIX:
"RAMPING UP THE DANGER!"
--IT DOESN'T LOOK LIKE HE'LL BE A THREAT TO ANYONE.
WAIT, FRANK, LOOK--HE'S STILL BREATHING!

LATER...
WE GOT THERE JUST IN TIME.
WHOEVER DID THAT BEAT HIM UP HARD--BUT HE SHOULD BE FINE.
UNLESS SHE IS THE BEST ACTRESS IN THE WHOLE WORLD--
--I DON'T THINK IT WAS HER.
I AGREE. SHE IS PRETTY BROKEN UP.
THAT'S IT-- I QUIT!
THAT'S JUST CRAZY TALK, PINKSHADE.
YOU'VE COME TOO FAR AND WORKED TOO HARD TO GIVE UP NOW.
DEX IS RIGHT.
THINK HOW DISAPPOINTED MR. MOTO WOULD BE IF HE HEARD.

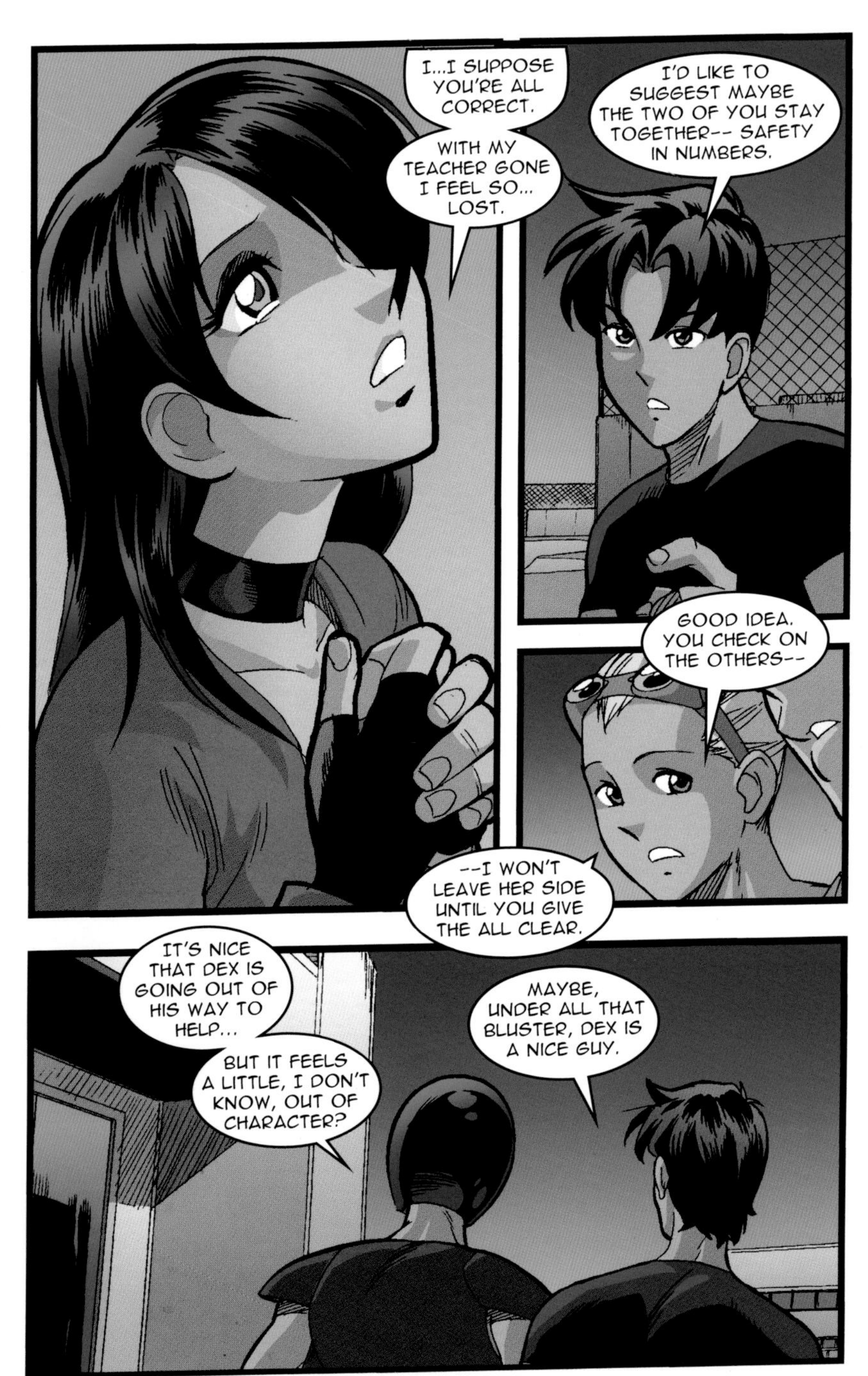
I...I SUPPOSE YOU'RE ALL CORRECT.
WITH MY TEACHER GONE I FEEL SO... LOST.
I'D LIKE TO SUGGEST MAYBE THE TWO OF YOU STAY TOGETHER-- SAFETY IN NUMBERS.
GOOD IDEA. YOU CHECK ON THE OTHERS--
--I WON'T LEAVE HER SIDE UNTIL YOU GIVE THE ALL CLEAR.
IT'S NICE THAT DEX IS GOING OUT OF HIS WAY TO HELP...
BUT IT FEELS A LITTLE, I DON'T KNOW, OUT OF CHARACTER?
MAYBE, UNDER ALL THAT BLUSTER, DEX IS A NICE GUY.

MAYBE.
THIS IS WRAITH'S TRAILER. LET'S HOPE WE REACHED HIM BE-FORE HE LEFT FOR--
KRASH
SOUNDS LIKE A STRUGGLE GOING ON IN THERE.
WHICH MEANS NO ONE IS GOING TO ANSWER IF WE KNOCK.
I HOPE WRAITH WILL PARDON MY MANNERS.
WHAM
INCREDIBLE!
THESE TWO DON'T KNOW WHEN TO STOP!

CHAPTER SEVEN:
"ONE2ONE!"
THIS IS NO TIME FOR A JOKE, JOE--WE NEED TO SEPARATE THEM BEFORE WRAITH IS HURT!
I WASN'T REALLY JOKING, BUT OKAY.

ENOUGH, COURAGE! YOU'RE GOING TO KILL HIM!
THAT'S WHAT HE PLANNED TO DO TO ME--I'M JUST DOING IT FIRST!
AND I SUPPOSE YOU HAVE PROOF OF THAT?

OF COURSE, HE DOESN'T...
WHEN I BEAT HIM IT'S GOING TO BE ON THE COURSE!

DO YOU WANT TO EXPLAIN WHAT'S GOING ON HERE?
WHAT'S TO EXPLAIN...?

RIDES ARE BEING SABOTAGED-- PEOPLE ARE BEING SHOT AT AND STABBED.
IF THE AUTHORITIES WON'T PROTECT ME, I WILL!

YOU CAN'T JUST JUMP TO CONCLUSIONS. THE ASSAILANT COULD BE ANYONE!
FOR EXAMPLE, EVEN THOUGH HE WAS THREATENED...
DEX COULD HAVE BEEN WORKING WITH A COLLABO-RATOR TO...

...TO....
IT *IS* DEX!

BY WORKING TOGETHER, MR. MOTO PROVIDED AN ALIBI FOR DEX.
AND DEX REPAID HIM BY NEARLY BEATING HIM TO DEATH.
AND AFTER MR. MOTO MADE IT A POINT TO SHOOT AT DEX WITHOUT ACTUALLY HITTING HIM!
I'M CONCERNED ABOUT PINKSHADE--WE LEFT HER ALONE WITH DEX!
NOT FOR LONG!
BAM
LONG ENOUGH, APPARENTLY.
THE DOOR WAS STILL LOCKED...
DEX SNEAKED HER OUT THROUGH THE TRAPDOOR IN THE FLOOR!

CHAPTER EIGHT: "THE LABYRINTH!"

HERE...
...I GRABBED THESE FROM PINKSHADE'S TRAILER. THEY ARE HER SPARE BOARDS.

I KNOW THE RIDE IS FUN, BUT KEEP YOUR EYES OPEN.
THERE'S A KILLER DOWN HERE WITH US -- I HAVEN'T FORGOTTEN.

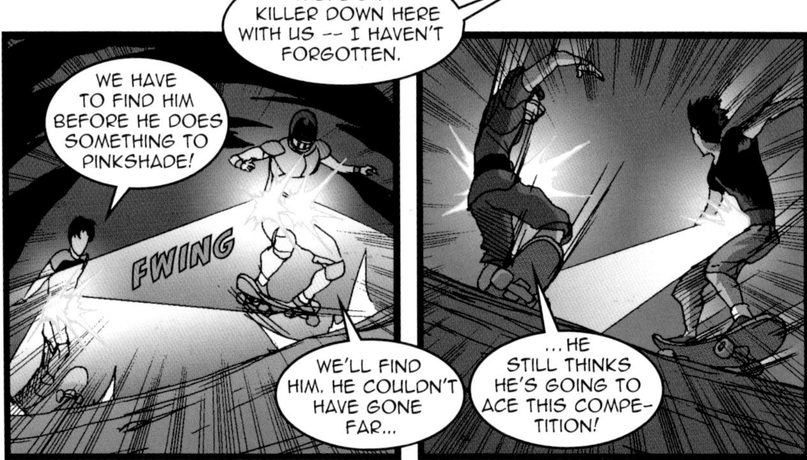
WE HAVE TO FIND HIM BEFORE HE DOES SOMETHING TO PINKSHADE!
FWING
WE'LL FIND HIM. HE COULDN'T HAVE GONE FAR...
...HE STILL THINKS HE'S GOING TO ACE THIS COMPE-TITION!

BECAUSE I AM...!
SKITCH
SKID

...NO MATTER WHO I HAVE TO KILL TO WALK AWAY WITH THE PRIZE THAT IS RIGHTFULLY MINE!
J-JOE... FRANK...
H-HELP ME, PLEASE!

THIS IS FRANK, PINKSHADE.
DON'T WORRY, WE'LL GET YOU OUT OF THIS.

I HAVE TO DISAGREE, FRANK.
YOU SEE, I'VE BEEN TRAINING FOR THIS DAY MY WHOLE LIFE...
"...IT WAS THAT DETERMINATION THAT CAUGHT THE ATTENTION OF MR. MOTO.
"HE SAW GREATNESS IN ME.
"A DRIVE THAT HE REALIZED PINKSHADE DID NOT POSSESS.
"HIS PLAN WAS TO HELP ME WIN...
"...AND TOGETHER WE'D GO ON TO WIN THE WORLDWIDE COMPETITION."

BUT WHEN HE REALIZED I WAS GOING TO KILL PINKSHADE --
--THE OLD MAN WENT SOFT. I HAD TO BETRAY HIM.
HE DIDN'T WANT ME DEAD?

NOW STEP OUT FROM BEHIND THOSE LIGHTS, HARDY BOYS!
I'LL KILL HER IF YOU DON'T. NOW!
I SAID "NOW!"

IS THIS "NOW" ENOUGH?
KRAK
WHA--?!

HOW...?!
I WAS HOLDING BOTH LIGHTS WHILE JOE GOT BESIDE YOU.

JOE, WE HAVE TO GET TO THE CONTEST!
IT'S YOUR TURN TO COMPETE.
I'M JUST GLAD WE STOPPED THE KILLER.

CHAPTER NINE: "BOOM!"
DID IT EVER OCCUR TO YOU, DEX, THAT YOU MIGHT HAVE WON BASED ON YOUR NATURAL SKILLS AND TRAINING?
OH, SHUT-UP. IT'S NOT BAD ENOUGH THAT YOU CAUGHT ME?

PINKSHADE TOLD US WHAT HAPPENED.
WE'LL TAKE HIM FROM HERE, MR. HARDY.
THANK YOU, OFFICERS.
HEH HEH

YOU'RE PRETTY HAPPY FOR A GUY WHO IS GOING TO JAIL FOR A LONG TIME.
HA HA!

BECAUSE I'LL HAVE MY REVENGE ON YOU AND YOUR BROTHER.
I REPLACED HIS BOARD WITH ONE MADE OF PLASTIQUE EXPLOSIVES.
WHEN HE LANDS AFTER HIS JUMP...?
CLAK
BOOM!
AND YOU'RE TOO LATE TO STOP IT!
TOO LATE! HA HA HA HA!

JUST IN TIME, FRANK!
NOOOO!
YOU ALMOST MISSED YOUR BROTHER'S JUMP.

I NEED TO BORROW THIS-- THANKS!
WHA--?!
FRANK, YOU CAN'T GO IN THERE!
NO WAY THIS IS GOING TO WORK--
--BUT WHAT OTHER CHOICE DO I HAVE?!

IS THAT... FRANK?
THAT'S CRAZY-- BUT HE MUST BE DOING IT FOR A REASON!

JOE--
JUMP!
NOW--
TRUST ME!
DON'T I
ALWAYS?
UNBELIEVABLE!
WOOHOO!
AMAZING!

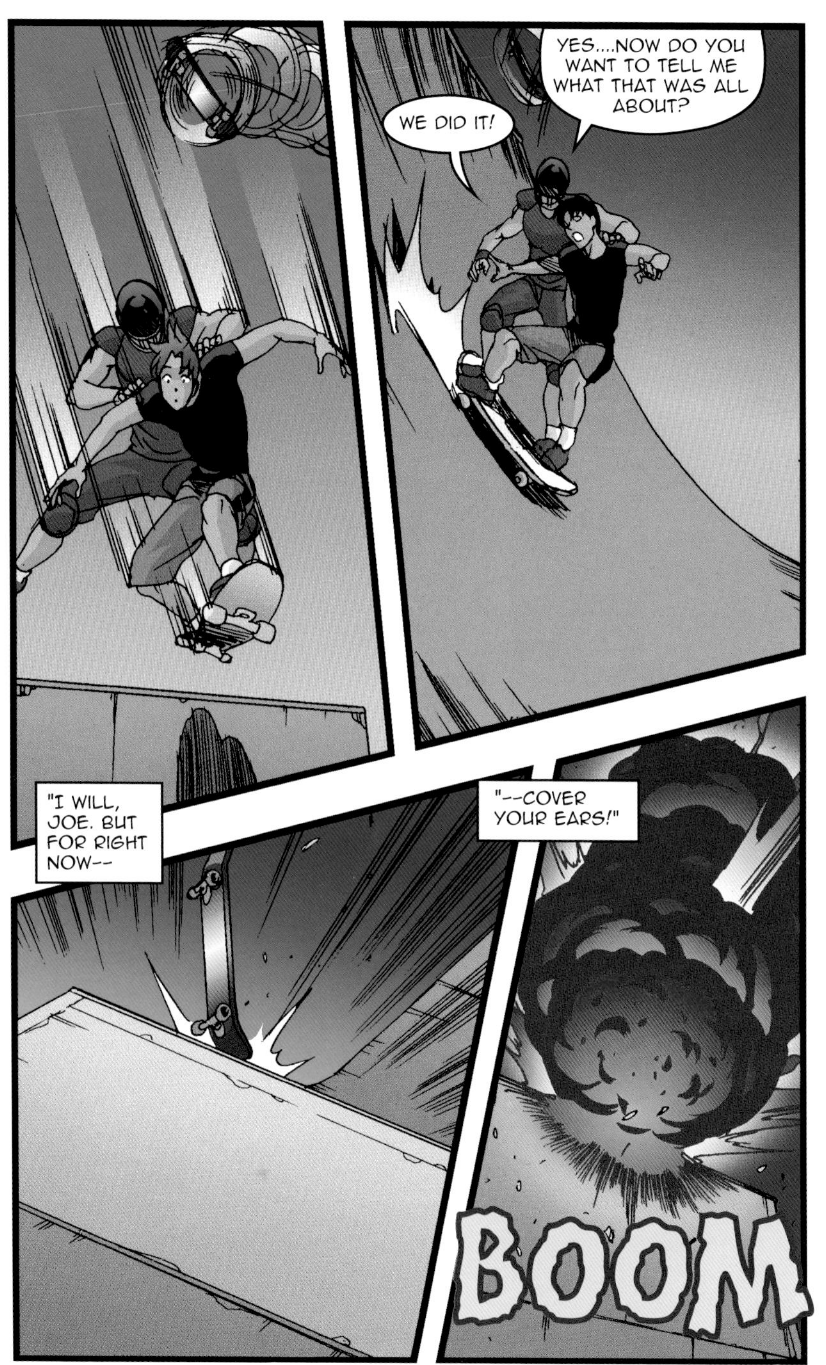
WE DID IT!
YES....NOW DO YOU WANT TO TELL ME WHAT THAT WAS ALL ABOUT?
"I WILL, JOE. BUT FOR RIGHT NOW--
"--COVER YOUR EARS!"
BOOM

TAKE A BOW, "HARDCASE"!
THEY THINK IT WAS ALL PART OF THE SHOW?
YEAH!
HARDCASE! HARDCASE!
HARDY BOYS ROCK!

IF I HADN'T SEEN THAT WITH MY OWN EYES...!
YOU TWO HAVE MAD SKILLS!
HOW MANY TIMES DID YOU REHEARSE THAT?!
HONESTLY, IT WAS JUST A FLUKE.
I CAN'T BELIEVE WE DIDN'T BREAK EVERY RULE IN THE BOOK!

ACTUALLY, I'M SAD TO SAY, YOU DID. THIS WAS A SOLO BOARD COMPETITION. I HAVE TO DISQUALIFY YOU.

AND I'M AFRAID WE'RE GOING TO HAVE TO POSTPONE THE FINAL ROUND FOR A WEEK--WHILE THE TRACK IS REPAIRED.

THE NATIONAL SKATEBOARDING CHAMPIONSHIP WINNER IS...

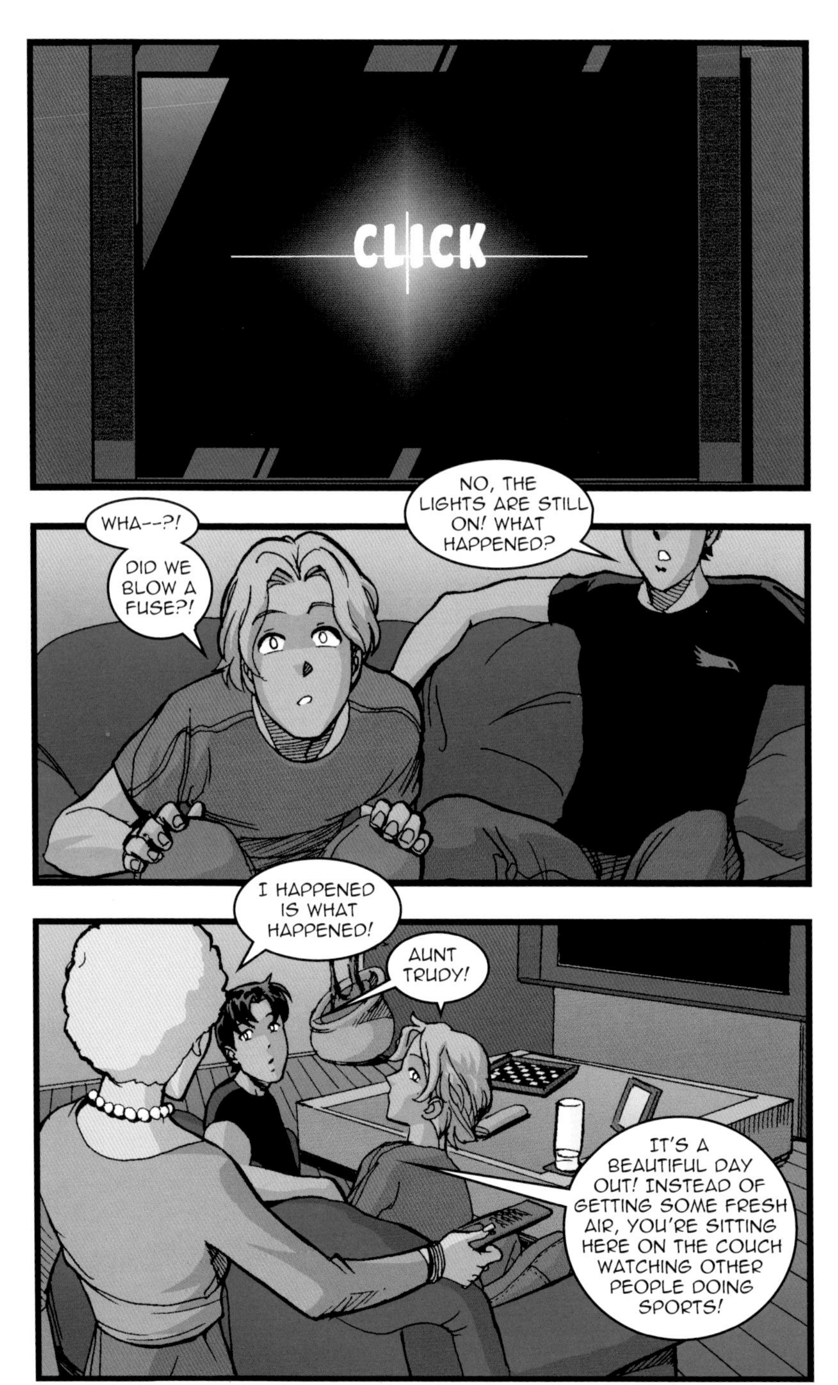
CLICK
WHA--?!
DID WE BLOW A FUSE?!
NO, THE LIGHTS ARE STILL ON! WHAT HAPPENED?
I HAPPENED IS WHAT HAPPENED!
AUNT TRUDY!
IT'S A BEAUTIFUL DAY OUT! INSTEAD OF GETTING SOME FRESH AIR, YOU'RE SITTING HERE ON THE COUCH WATCHING OTHER PEOPLE DOING SPORTS!

SOMETIMES YOU NEED TO GET YOUR BLOOD PUMPING.
GOOD POINT!
YOU'RE ALWAYS LOOKING OUT FOR US, AUNT T.
IT'S ONLY FAIR WE RETURN THE FAVOR.
ARE YOU THINKING WHAT I'M THINKING?

SOON...
YOU'RE A NATURAL.
THIS IS A LOT MORE FUN THAN IT LOOKS ON TELEVISION!
AT THIS RATE...

...WE'LL BE ABLE TO ENTER YOU INTO NEXT YEAR'S CONTEST!
YOU'LL NEED A NICKNAME.
HOW ABOUT... AUNT TNT!
HA HA
HA
HA HA

"TO DIE OR NOT TO DIE?"
FRANK--LOOK OUT!
I SEE IT, JOE! I'M SURPRISED IT HAS COME TO THIS-- BUT I SEE IT!

BLAM
BLAM
BLAM
YOU PUNKS! I HAD A GOOD RACKET GOING ON HERE!

I KNOW WE'RE ALWAYS AT RISK WHENEVER WE TAKE A CASE--
BUT I WASN'T EXPECTING IT ALL TO END AT A MINIATURE GOLF COURSE!
PTING
PTING
GRANTED OUR SITUATION IS GRIM--
BUT LET'S NOT RUSH TO EBAY TO ORDER TOMBSTONES JUST YET.
CHAPTER ONE:
"A HORROR IN ONE!"

DO YOU HAVE A PLAN?
WHO AM I KIDDING-- YOU ALWAYS HAVE A PLAN!
CREDIT WHERE CREDIT IS DUE.
PTING PTING

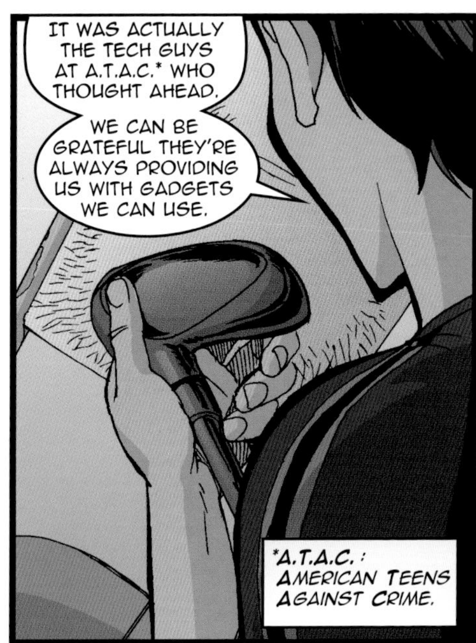
IT WAS ACTUALLY THE TECH GUYS AT A.T.A.C.* WHO THOUGHT AHEAD.
WE CAN BE GRATEFUL THEY'RE ALWAYS PROVIDING US WITH GADGETS WE CAN USE.
*A.T.A.C.: AMERICAN TEENS AGAINST CRIME.

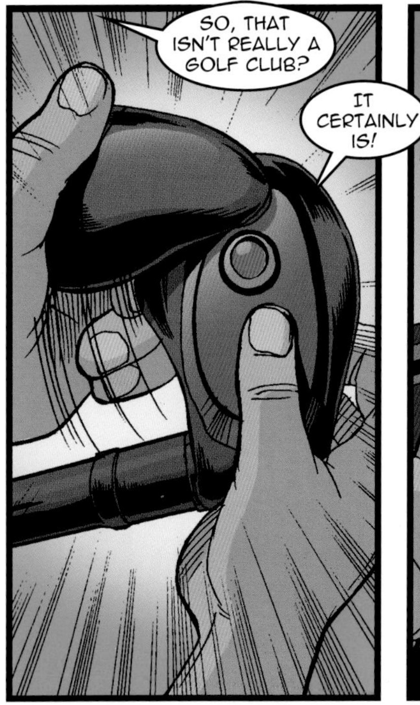
SO, THAT ISN'T REALLY A GOLF CLUB?
IT CERTAINLY IS!

BUT IT'S ALSO SO MUCH MORE.
CLICK

"IT ALSO TRANSMITS A SIGNAL, JOE..."
BEEP
"...TO THE GOLF BALL THAT'S MORE THAN A GOLF BALL."

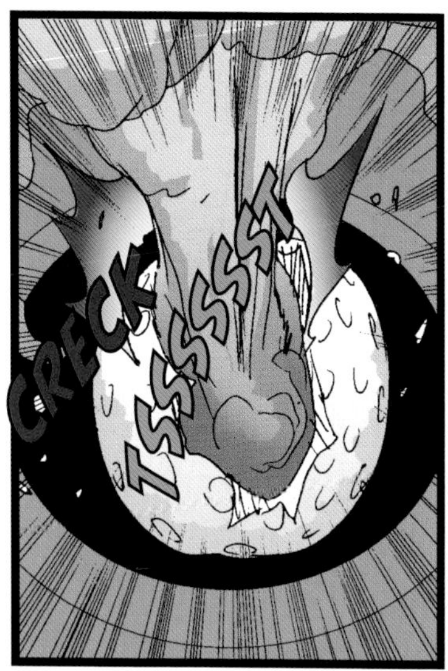
CRECK
TSSSSSSST

WHAT THE--?!
COUGH COUGH
GAK!
FWOOOOSH

THAT ONLY TOOK SECONDS AND HE'S OUT LIKE A LIGHT.
THE PREFERRED POSITION OF ALL CRAZED GUNMEN.
WHICH GIVES US A CHANCE...

...TO CONFIRM OUR SUSPICIONS ABOUT THIS PLACE.
CREAK

THE HIDDEN CAMERA...JUST WHERE WE THOUGHT IT WAS.
SO THAT'S HOW HE DID IT?
HE USED THE SURVEILLANCE TO...

...SPY ON ALL HIS CUSTOMERS.
HE'D SIT HERE AND LISTEN TO THEIR PRIVATE CONVERSATIONS.
WE KNEW IT COULDN'T BE A COINCIDENCE THAT ALL THOSE HOUSES WERE BEING BROKEN INTO WHILE PEOPLE WERE HERE FOR THE NIGHT.
EXACTLY, SHERIFF COLLIG! HE'D SIT HERE MAKING NOTES--
--AND SELL THE PRIVATE INFORMATION TO A LOCAL BURGLAR RING.
•Mike Russo (Beware of dog)
•Barry Dutter (writer, lonely)
•Joan Vento Hall (lawyer, married)

I'VE BEEN IN LAW ENFORCEMENT FOR MANY YEARS.
AND I'M STILL AMAZED AT ALL THE WAYS BAD PEOPLE CAN THINK OF TO TAKE ADVANTAGE OF OTHERS.
YOU'D THINK FOLKS WOULD BE SAFE ENJOYING A NIGHT PLAYING MINIATURE GOLF.
MOST COURSES ARE COMPLETELY SAFE.

NOT ONLY DO YOU DO GREAT WORK, YOU HAVE A GREAT ATTITUDE.
THANKS, SIR. WE APPRECIATE THAT.

WHAT DO YOU SAY, FRANK--A QUICK ROUND?
HONESTLY? I'LL BE HAPPY IF I NEVER SEE ANOTHER GOLF CLUB EVER AGAIN!

CHAPTER TWO: "ALL THE WORLD'S A STAGE"

AWESOME!
PLEASE. NOW YOU'RE ALL BEING SILLY.
BRAVO!
CLAP CLAP

ACTUALLY, I HAVE TO AGREE WITH YOUR CLASSMATES, FRANK.
YOUR PERFORMANCE WAS THOUGHTFUL AND ENERGIZED.
YOU MAKE AN EXCELLENT HAMLET.

THANK YOU, MISS WHITE.
IT'S ALMOST FUNNY HOW ALL MY A.T.A.C. TRAINING IN UNDERCOVER WORK WITH JOE--
--GAVE ME THE SAME SKILLS I NEED TO APPLY TO ACTING.
NOT THAT I CAN SHARE THAT WITH THE CLASS.

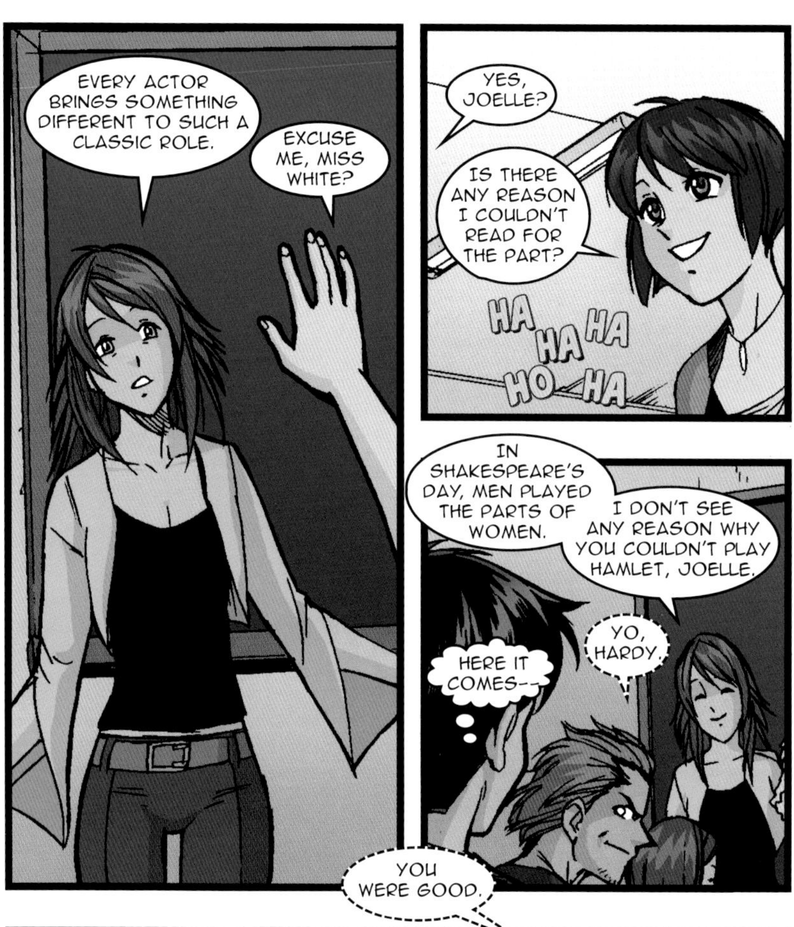
EVERY ACTOR BRINGS SOMETHING DIFFERENT TO SUCH A CLASSIC ROLE.
EXCUSE ME, MISS WHITE?
YES, JOELLE?
IS THERE ANY REASON I COULDN'T READ FOR THE PART?
HA HA HA HO HA
IN SHAKESPEARE'S DAY, MEN PLAYED THE PARTS OF WOMEN.
I DON'T SEE ANY REASON WHY YOU COULDN'T PLAY HAMLET, JOELLE.
YO, HARDY.
HERE IT COMES--

YOU WERE GOOD.
?!
THANKS, BRIAN.

BRRRINNNNG
YOU'RE CLEARLY INTO ACTING.

WHY DON'T YOU TRY OUT FOR THE SCHOOL PLAY?
YEAH, RIGHT.

THIS CLASS IS JUST AN ELECTIVE.
I WOULDN'T BE CAUGHT DEAD HANGING AROUND WITH DRAMA KIDS.
YOUR SECRET IS SAFE WITH ME.

IT BETTER BE!
OH, HEY. HI.
YOU'RE A NATURAL ON STAGE, FRANK.
IN FACT, I WAS HOPING TO ASK YOU A FAVOR!
SOON...
YOU WANT ME TO WHAT--?!
BE MY ACTING PARTNER--
--IN THE ANNUAL ALL STATE COM-PETITION!

I'M HONORED YOU WOULD ASK ME, JOELLE.
SO, IS THAT A YES?!

YOU NEED SOMEONE SERIOUS ABOUT BEING AN ACTOR.
I'D ONLY HOLD YOU BACK.

GOOD LUCK, THOUGH.
NO, KEEP IT!

MORE IMPORTANTLY, KEEP AN OPEN MIND!
OKAY, I'LL TRY.
BYE!
THAT IS ONE BEAUTIFUL GIRL.

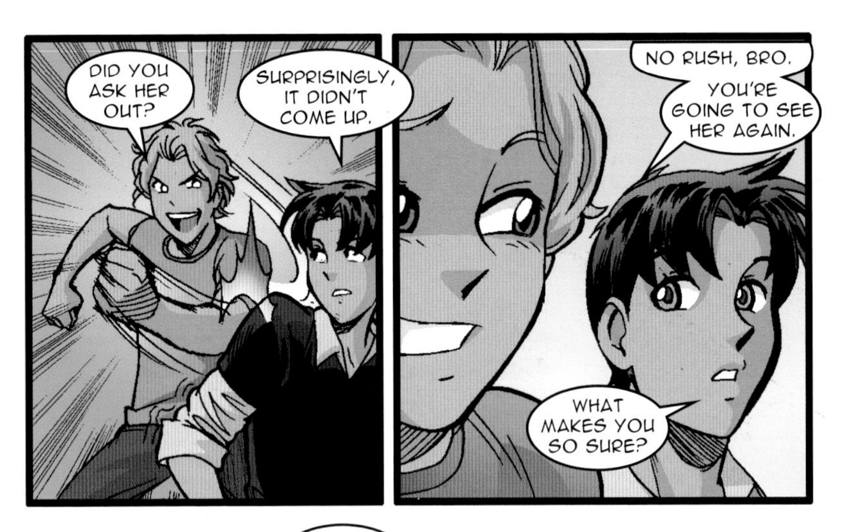
DID YOU ASK HER OUT?
SURPRISINGLY, IT DIDN'T COME UP.
NO RUSH, BRO.
YOU'RE GOING TO SEE HER AGAIN.
WHAT MAKES YOU SO SURE?

JUST A HUNCH.
TO DIE OR NOT TO DIE ?
THAT, AND I FOUND THIS GAME CARTRIDGE IN MY LOCKER.

LATER THAT NIGHT...
...AT THE BAYPORT HOME OF THE HARDY BROTHERS...

JUST ONCE I'D LIKE TO DO THIS WITH A BIG TUB OF POPCORN.
THIS ISN'T A MOVIE, JOE-- IT'S OUR NEXT CASE.
WE NEED TO TAKE IT SERIOUSLY.
WOW, FRANK. YOU GET CRANKY WHEN YOU'RE IN LOVE.
WEBA

A.T.A.C.

WHAT ARE YOU TALKING ABOUT? I'M NOT--

GREETINGS, HARDY BOYS. THANK YOU ONCE AGAIN FOR YOUR SERVICE TO AMERICAN TEENS AGAINST CRIME.

ONLY THIS YEAR, IT HAS BECOME DECIDEDLY DEADLY.
A STUDENT HAS ALMOST DIED--

--WHILE OTHERS WERE ONLY IN-CAPACITATED.

TENACITY MIGHT BE A VIRTUE IN ANY ACTOR--BUT THIS PERSON WANTS TO WIN AT ANY PRICE.

ONE OF YOUR FELLOW STUDENTS HAS EARNED A SPOT IN THE CONTEST.
HER NAME IS JOELLE RINKER, AND WE WANT YOU TO ENSURE HER SAFETY--

--WHILE YOU SUSS OUT THE PERSON RESPONSIBLE FOR THE CRIMES.
FRANK? ARE YOU COOL WITH THIS?

I MEAN, MAYBE YOU'RE TOO CLOSE TO THIS CASE? WE CAN--
I'LL BE FINE, JOE.WE BETTER GET PACKED.

"THE HOLLYWOOD BOWL IN CALIFORNIA IS AN OUTDOOR THEATER.
"WE'LL NEED LOTS OF LIGHT WEATHER CLOTHING."

YOUR NAME?
FRANK HARDY. BAYPORT HIGH.
AND YOUR NAME?

I'M NOT REGISTERING.
I'M JUST JOE HARDY, PRODUCTION ASSISTANT.

EVEN THOUGH WE EXAMINED THE LAYOUT OF THE BUILDING ON THE INTERNET, LET'S TAKE A LOOK AROUND AND--
YOU DIRTY DOG--!
YOU TRICKED ME!
UM--
YOU WERE GOING TO COME ALL ALONG!
ACTUALLY--
HEH HA
UM, HAVE YOU MET MY BROTHER?
DON'T DRAG ME INTO THIS.

THIS IS--

?!
MWAH

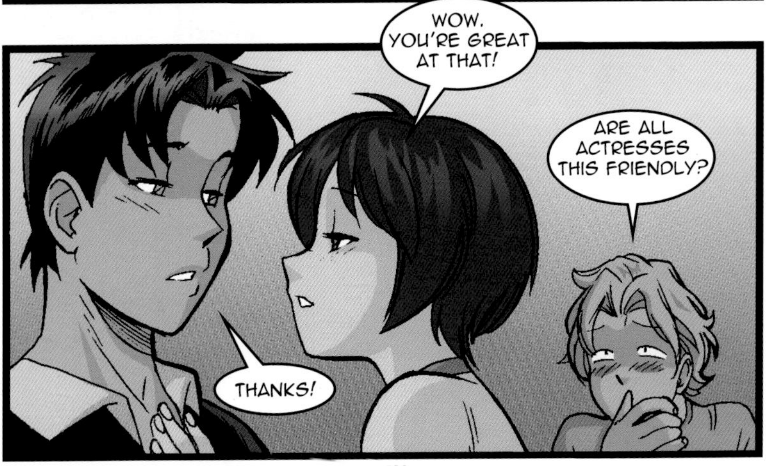
WOW. YOU'RE GREAT AT THAT!
THANKS!
ARE ALL ACTRESSES THIS FRIENDLY?

WHAT? OH, WAIT--YOU DON'T THINK I WAS--??
LOOK AT THE SCENE WE HAVE TO DO TOGETHER. THERE IS A KISS!
I WAS JUST REHEARSING!

OH. YEAH, NO. I GUESSED THAT.
I SO MADE A MISTAKE BY JOIN-ING THE FOOTBALL TEAM.

I'M OFF TO WARDROBE! I'LL SEE YOU LATER, FRANK!
ACTORS HAVE WAY MORE FUN THAN VOLUNTEERS.
WANT TO SWITCH?
MR. HARDY, LET ME GET THE DOOR FOR YOU.
A STAR OF YOUR MAGNITUDE SHOULDN'T HAVE TO OPEN--
YEAH, YEAH, YEAH.

IT'S DARK BACK HERE.
THE BACKSTAGE AREA IS ENCLOSED TO PROTECT FROM THE WEATHER.
WE'VE GOT TO SECURE THIS WHOLE BUILDING IF WE WANT TO KEEP EVERY-ONE SAFE.
FRANK-- LOOK OUT!
WHAT'S WRONG?

CHAPTER THREE:
"EXIT STAGE LEFT--
FOREVER!"
THAT STAGE LIGHT?!
SMASH

LOOK, UP THERE--IN THE CATWALK!
I CAN'T MAKE OUT ANY IDENTIFYING DETAILS, IT'S TOO DARK.
ROUND ONE TO THE KILLER!
HALF A ROUND, ANYWAY.
SINCE YOU DID SAVE MY LIFE.
I'M A BIG FAN.

LATER...

THIS LITTLE FIELD TRIP MAKES ME UNCOMFORTABLE.
I'LL SAY, THE KILLER COULD BE ANYWHERE.

HERE'S THE BUS TO TAKE US TO THE PLAY.
LET'S SPLIT UP--COVER MORE GROUND.

THERE YOU ARE!
OH, HEY.
DON'T EVEN PRETEND YOU'RE NOT SIT-TING WITH ME!
THAT'S ONE WAY TO KEEP AN EYE ON HER.
THIS IS PERFECT--WE CAN PRACTICE OUR PARTS FOR TONIGHT'S CONTEST.
AND NO MORE KISSING. I PROMISE.
MOSTLY.

HI, MRS. MARS. I'M JOE HARDY.
ARE YOU CONCERNED WITH THE SAFETY OF THE STUDENTS, CONSIDERING WHAT'S BEEN HAPPENING DURING THE RUN UPS?

OH, PISH! THEY'RE A BUNCH OF DRAMA QUEENS WORRYING OVER NOTHING AT ALL!

IN MY DAY, WE KNEW-- THE SHOW MUST GO ON!

THAT'S FINE.
BUT NOT OVER MY DEAD BODY, THANK YOU VERY MUCH.

THE THEATER HAS ALWAYS BEEN A DANGEROUS PLACE.
THAT IS WHY GARGOYLES WERE PLACED AROUND THOSE BUILDINGS IN ANCIENT TIMES--
--TO PROTECT FROM EVIL SPIRITS.

AND YOU ARE--?
XIAO LOONG. IT STANDS FOR LITTLE DRAGON IN CHINESE.
IT WAS ALSO BRUCE LEE'S ORIGINAL NAME.

"NOW YOU MUST SUFFER FOR YOUR AFFRONT TO MY PERSONAGE!
"SUFFER AS NONE HAS E'ER BEFORE YOU!"

WOW, YOU'RE GOOD.
SOK
YOU'RE NOT JUST SAYING THAT?

HA! I AM TOO TIRED TO HELP YOU FISH FOR COMPLIMENTS.
WAS UP... ALL NIGHT...
YAWN
...MEMORIZING LINES.

CAN I TELL YOU A SECRET...?
PLEASE.

I DON'T USUALLY LIKE ACTORS.
OH. CAN I TELL YOU A SECRET?
PLEASE.

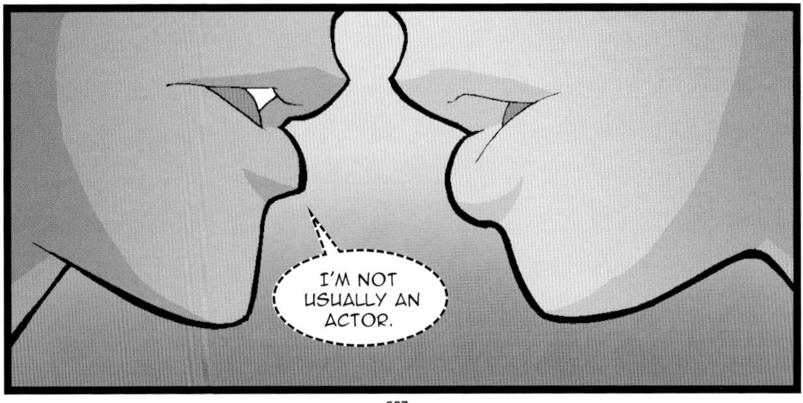
I'M NOT USUALLY AN ACTOR.

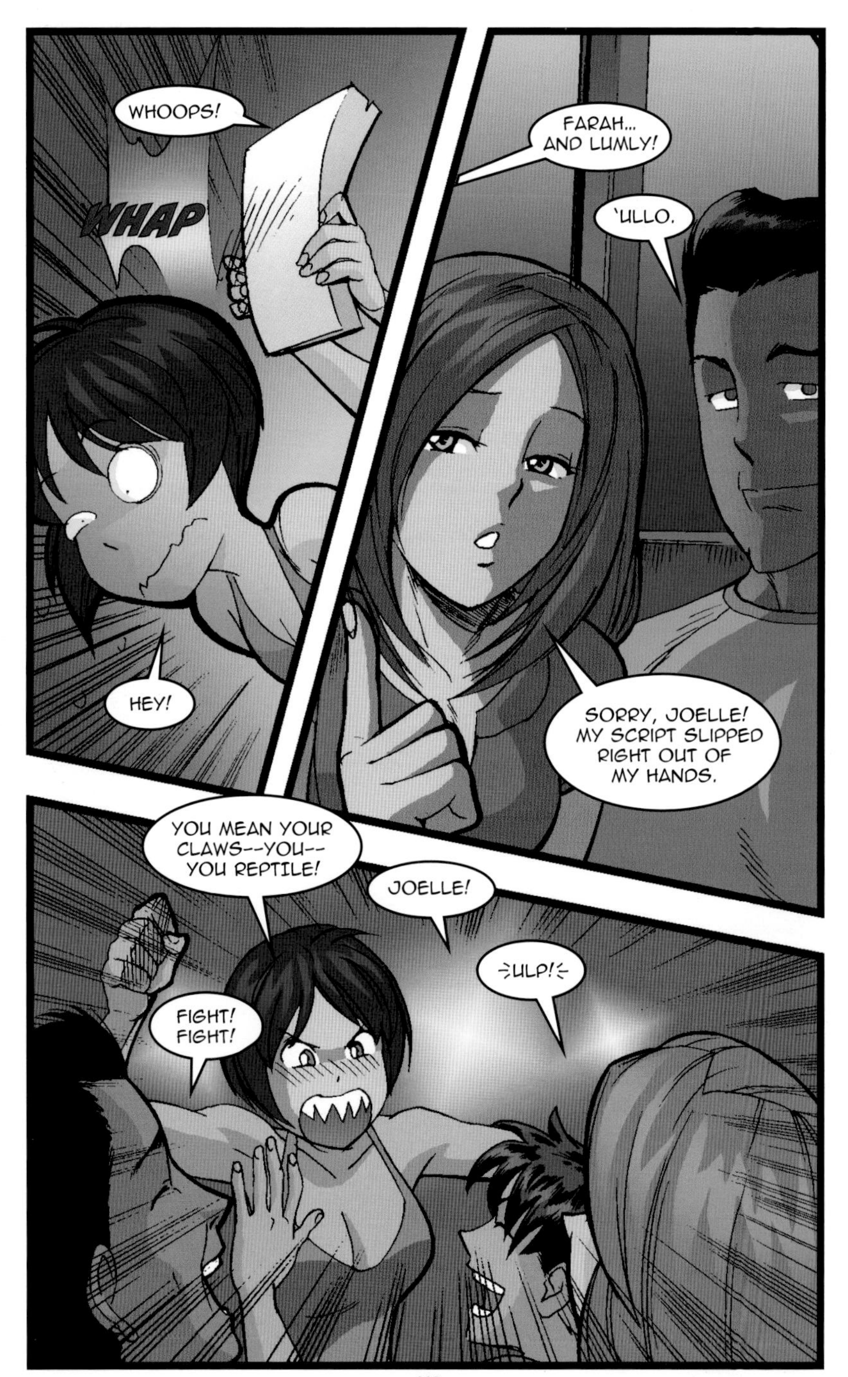
WHOOPS!
WHAP
HEY!
FARAH... AND LUMLY!
`ULLO.
SORRY, JOELLE! MY SCRIPT SLIPPED RIGHT OUT OF MY HANDS.
YOU MEAN YOUR CLAWS--YOU--YOU REPTILE!
JOELLE!
ULP!
FIGHT! FIGHT!

IIIEEEEEE!
HUNH?!
WHA--?!
...MERCIFULLY THE OTHER DRIVERS ARE PULLING OVER!
JOE, WHAT'S WRONG?
APPARENTLY, THE BRAKES!
I CAN'T STOP THE BUS...

IT'S ALL I CAN DO TO KEEP US ON THE ROAD--
-- I CAN'T PULL THE EMERGENCY BRAKE!
LEAVE THAT TO US!

EVERYONE HOLD ON TIGHT!

YANK

CHAPTER FOUR:
"TAKING THE SHOW ON THE ROAD!"
SCCHHRREEEEEEEEE

B-BUMP
TH-BUMP
B-BUMP

AAAAH!
HOW WE DOING?
WE'RE ALL ALIVE. SO FAR.
IIIIEEE!
SHHRRRUSHHHH
JOE, WE MISSED THAT TREE BY INCHES!
CLOSE ENOUGH, FRANK!

AFTER THE AUTHORITIES HAVE BEEN SUMMONED...
THIS SEEMS TO RULE OUT ANYONE WHO WAS ON BOARD.
TRUE. KILLERS ARE UNLIKELY TO PUT THEMSELVES AT RISK. BUT STILL--

YOUR QUICK ACTION SAVED A LOT OF LIVES TODAY, BOYS.
WE WERE LUCKY. WHOEVER MESSED WITH THE BRAKES MUST NOT HAVE HAD ENOUGH TIME TO FINISH THE JOB.
POL

MRS. MARS, YOU MIGHT WANT TO CONSIDER CANCELING THIS COMPETITION.
I'M AFRAID I MIGHT AGREE WITH THAT SENTIMENT.
BUT--
YOU CAN'T! WE'VE PRACTICED YEARS TO GET HERE!
SHE'S RIGHT! WE DESERVE THE CHANCE TO WIN!
I UNDERSTAND THAT--BUT YOUR SAFETY--

LOOK, THE BACK-UP BUS THAT WAS ORDERED IS HERE!
OFFICER--YOU DON'T WANT ME TO CRY, DO YOU?
I'M SO S-SAD.
I DON'T WANT ANYONE TO BE SAD, BUT --

WHAT HAPPENED TO THE SHOW MUST GO ON, MRS. MARS?
YOU'RE NOT GOING TO LET PARA-NOIA STAND IN THE WAY OF TRADITION, ARE YOU?
HMP

CURTAIN'S UP, LADIES AND GENTLEMAN!
WE'VE GOT A SHOW TO DO, AND DAGNABBIT, WE'RE GOING TO DO IT!

COME ON, FRANK--LET'S REHEARSE ON THE BUS!
SURE THING, JOELLE.
JOE--?
BREAK A LEG, BRO!

THE NEXT MORNING...
NOOOOOOOO OOOOOOOO!

THEY CHANGED OUR PERFORMANCE RULES! WE'RE NOT PREPARED!
SOMEONE WANTS TO RUIN US!
THIS IS SO UNFAIR!
WE CAN IMPROVISE, JOELLE-- MAKE IT UP AS WE GO ALONG.

KNOCK KNOCK
TWO MINUTES TO SHOWTIME, KIDS!
GIVE US A MINUTE, JOE.

JOELLE, YOU'RE THE MOST TALENTED GIRL I'VE EVER MET.
WE'RE GOING TO BE FINE.

OH, FRANK-- YOU'RE RIGHT!
TOGETHER, WE CAN DO ANYTHING!

ONSTAGE...
AS YOU KNOW, "IMPROVISATION" CHALLENGES THE ACTOR TO THINK ON HIS FEET.
WORKING WITH ONLY A SCENARIO, YOU MUST MAKE UP THEIR CHARACTERS ON THE RUN!

YOUR PLAN WORKED, FARAH. NO WAY IS JOELLE PREPARED FOR THIS.
MRS. MARS WAS EASY TO MANIPULATE. NOW SHUSH--

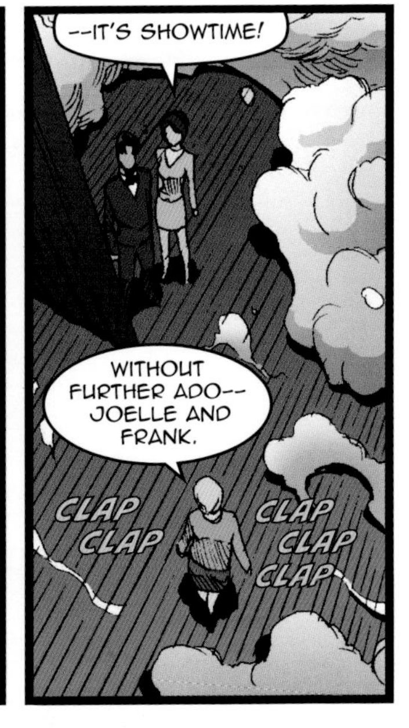
--IT'S SHOWTIME!
WITHOUT FURTHER ADO-- JOELLE AND FRANK.
CLAP CLAP
CLAP CLAP CLAP

ENRIQUE-- THE FOG GOES ON FOR MILES! HOW WILL WE EVER REACH THE SHIP IN TIME?
DON'T WORRY, YOUR MAJESTY--
--WE WOULDN'T BE MUCH OF A REBELLION IF WE CAVED AT THE FIRST SIGHT OF ADVERSITY, WOULD WE?

SPEAKING OF SIGHT--
--BEWARE THAT ALVURIAN TONGUE PIT!
GOOD SAVE!
HEH HA
HE HA

JUST AS YOU SAVED MY HEART WITH YOUR SMILE.
ENRIQUE-- WE'RE SOLDIERS, WE DON'T DARE!
THAT'S NONSENSE, YOUR MAJESTY--
--IF WE DON'T FIGHT FOR LOVE--
--WE FIGHT FOR NOTHING AT ALL.

Y-YOU'RE RIGHT, OF COURSE.
BUT LOVE AND HONOR--DOES NOT ONE TRUMP THE OTHER?
SNFF, SNFF

YOU'RE ROOTING FOR ME, REMEMBER?!
RIGHT. SORRY.

I CAN'T BELIEVE SHE'S GOING TO PULL THIS OFF!
SPRITZ TIZZ

WITHOUT LOVE, THERE IS NO HONOR.
WHICH IS WHY I HONOR YOU...WITH MY LOVE.

YEAH! WOO HOO!
AWESOME!
BRAVO! BRAVO!
CLAP CLAP
CLAP
CLAP

FRANK, YOU'RE GOOD.
WHO KNEW?

HOW'D SHE DO IT?!
YOU CAN STILL TAKE HER, FARAH. JUST STAY CALM AND--

FIIIIIIIRE!
OH MY GOSH! HELP! HELP!
FRANK, LOOK!
STAND BACK! I'LL GET THEM OUT OF THERE!
SOMEHOW.
HEAD'S UP, FRANK!
THANKS, JOE!

TOSSING ME THAT FIRE EXTINGUISHER WAS HELPFUL--
BUT I WONDER WHERE JOE WENT TO?
ONE OF THESE ROPES MUST CONTROL THE CURTAIN THAT IS IN FLAMES!
BUT MAN, THOSE ARE A LOT OF ROPES.
FWOOOSH
STAYING!
STAY BACK!

CHAPTER FIVE:
"IT'S CURTAINS FOR YOU, FRANK HARDY!"

I'VE PUT OUT THE SMOG MACHINE FIRE--
--BUT IF THE FLAMES JUMP FROM THIS CURTAIN TO ANOTHER--
--THIS WHOLE PLACE COULD GO UP!

FRANK-- STEP AWAY FROM THE CURTAINS!
I HAVE AN IDEA!
CLEAR!
THIS FIREMAN'S AXE OUGHT TO DO THE TRICK!
IF I CAN SEVER THE ROPES IN ONE SWING--
SHUNK

"--THE CURTAIN WILL COLLAPSE!"
THIS IS YOUR BIG EXIT, GUYS!
TH-THANKS!
OUPHF!

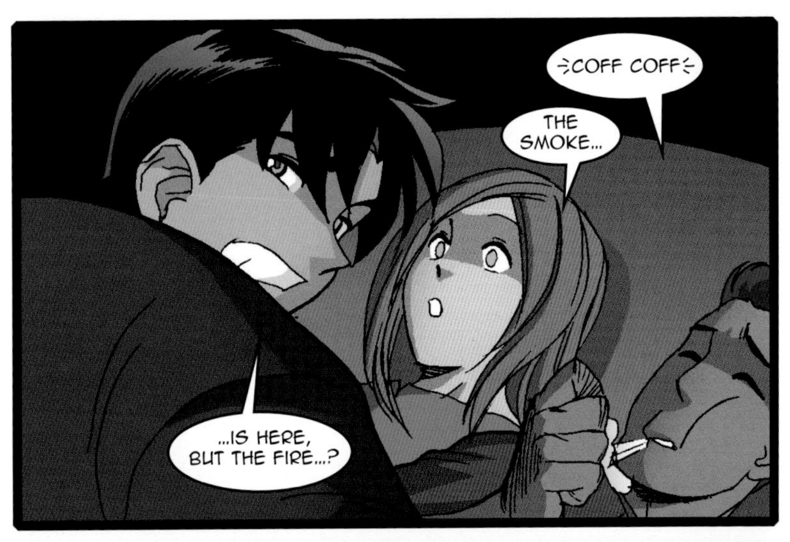
COFF COFF
THE SMOKE...
...IS HERE, BUT THE FIRE...?

...IS OUT! THE CURTAINS SMOTHERED THE FLAMES.
JUST AS I'D HOPED.
PERFECT. AND THANKS.

I GUESS YOU COULD SAY IT WAS CURTAINS FOR THE CURTAINS.
YOU COULD.
IF YOU HAD TO.

HMM. I'M AFRAID THE FOG MACHINE ISN'T GOING TO GIVE US ANY CLUES--
--AS TO WHETHER IT WAS DELIBERATELY SABOTAGED OR NOT.

YEAH, SORRY ABOUT THAT.
I GUESS I SMASHED THE EVIDENCE.
YEAH, BUT IT SAVED OUR LIVES SO IT'S--

EEEEEEEEEEEEEE
WHA--?!
IT SOUNDS LIKE FARAH!

YOU DID THAT ON PURPOSE!
YOU'RE TRYING TO TAKE THE SPOTLIGHT OFF OF ME!
THAT'S CRAZY! YOU'RE CRAZY!

JOELLE, THERE'S NO PROOF SHE HAD ANYTHING TO--
I DON'T NEED PROOF! I KNOW!
ARE YOU OKAY?
I AM. BUT SHE IS NUTS!

I'M NUTS?! FIRST YOU TRY TO RUIN MY SCENE WITH FRANK!
WHEN THAT DOESN'T WORK YOU TRY TO BURN THE PLACE DOWN!
I WAS IN THE FIRE-- HELLO!

WHY WOULD I RISK MY LIFE, WHEN ALL I HAVE TO DO IS ACT CIRCLES AROUND YOUR BONEY BOTTOM?!
GOOD IDEA!
LESS FIGHTING! MORE ACTING!

IT WOULD BE A SHAME IF YOU BOTH GOT KICKED OUT FOR FIGHTING, WOULDN'T IT?
YOU'RE RIGHT, OF COURSE...
YOU'RE THE BEST, FRANK HARDY!

...
WHO'D ARGUE THAT?
GRRR
HOT!

LATER, IN THE DRESSING ROOM...
HERE YOU GO, JOELLE. THIS SHOULD HELP YOU REST.
YOU... ROCK.

I'LL CHECK UP ON YOU LATER.
TH-THANKS...
GOOD...
...NIGH'...

SHE'S SO... BEAUTIFUL. SO FRAGILE.
COULD I BE... FALLING FOR HER?

THAT STRIKES ME AS A BAD IDEA.
I'M ON A CASE, NOT A DATE.
I NEED TO KEEP A CLEAR HEAD IF I'M GOING TO PROTECT HER.
FRANK, ARE YOU OKAY?
IT'S NOT LIKE YOU TO GET SO EMOTIONALLY INVOLVED WITH THE PEOPLE WE'RE TRYING TO HELP.

AND IT'S NOT LIKE YOU TO TRY MINDREADING.

I'M NOT TRYING TO PRY. I'M JUST--
--CONCERNED. AND I APPRECIATE IT, JOE.
I'M GOING TO BE FINE.

IT JUST STILL BOTHERS ME--THAT BUS CRASH COULD HAVE BEEN FATAL...FOR EVERYONE ON-BOARD.

SAME THING WITH THAT FIRE. IT WOULD HAVE BEEN IMPOSSIBLE TO CON-TAIN IF WE HADN'T STOPPED IT.

BUT IT DOESN'T MAKE SENSE.
LIKE THE KILLER DOESN'T CARE ABOUT HIS OR HER OWN SAFETY.

IT'S A PUZZLER, THAT'S FOR SURE.
BUT WE'VE SOLVED TOUGHER CASES BEFORE.
MAYBE... IT'S NOT AS TOUGH AS WE THINK IT IS. MAYBE THE ANSWER IS RIGHT IN FRONT--
IIIIIIIIIIIII-IEEEEEEE!

SOMEONE! ANYONE!
HELP!

CHAPTER SIX:
"WALK...
DON'T RUN!"
I THOUGHT I SAW JOELLE SLEEPWALKING!
BUT IF SHE MISSTEPS, SHE'LL BE KILLED!

THAT'S CRAZY! SOMEONE MUST HAVE LURED HER UP THERE!
WE'LL FIGURE OUT THE HOW AFTER WE GET HER DOWN!
I'LL TAKE THE STEPS UP AND SEE IF--
WAIT, FRANK!
?
GRAB THIS!
FWING
YANK
--AND HANG ON!

JOE WAS RIGHT-- THIS IS A LOT QUICKER!
BUT WILL I GET UP THERE IN TIME TO MAKE A DIF- FERENCE?
I'M CLOSE ENOUGH TO JUMP!
I DON'T DARE CALL OUT TO HER.
IF I STARTLE HER AWAKE SHE MIGHT TUMBLE OVER THE SIDE THAT MUCH SOONER!

NOOOOO! HE'S TOO LATE...!
IT'S NOT LOOKING GOOD.
C'MON, FRANK...

YOU'RE SAFE, JOELLE--JUST STAY CALM!
WHA--!?
FRANK-- WHAT HAPPENED?! WHERE AM I?!
SHE'S PANICKED!
SHE'S TWISTING AWAY!
FRANK WON'T LET GO.
JOE?

WOULD IT BE TOO CLICHE IF I SAID "MY HERO"?
THAT DEPENDS.
WOULD IT BE TOO CLICHE IF I SAID "I COULDN'T LIVE WITH MYSELF IF ANYTHING HAD HAPPENED TO YOU"?

IN A LITTLE BIT...
JOE, WHAT IF WE MADE A MISTAKE?
BY CONVINCING MRS. MARS TO KEEP THIS CONTEST GOING --
--SO WE CAN TRACK DOWN THE PERSON RESPONSIBLE?
SEEMS TO ME THE ALTERNATIVE IS WE LET THE PERSON GET AWAY WITH EVERYTHING THEY'VE DONE SO FAR.

NO ONE WANTS TO SEE THAT HAPPEN.
NO... YOU'RE RIGHT. YOU'RE RIGHT.

THE NEXT MORNING...
IN ACTING, YOUR BODY IS THE TOOL YOU USE TO PRACTICE YOUR CRAFT
YOGA IS A WAY TO FINE TUNE YOUR BODY.

FARAH, HAVE YOU SEEN JOELLE THIS MORNING?
I HAVEN'T EVEN URNN SEEN MY BREAKFAST YET.

MR. HARDY, CAN YOU CHECK ON XIAO LOONG'S WHERE-ABOUTS?
SURE THING, MRS. MARS. I LIVE TO SERVE.
HMMM...COULD XIAO BE OFF SOMEWHERE, PLANNING ANOTHER ASSAULT ON ONE OF HIS FELLOW ACTORS?
I GUESS I'LL FIND OUT AS SOON AS I FIND--

--HIM?!

XIAO LOONG--WHAT HAPPENED?!
HMMF MRMF RRMF!
SORRY I ASKED!
THOSE CABLES ATTACHED TO THE FENCE...
...MUST LEAD TO A WALL UNIT!
I NEED HELP BACKSTAGE--
KLICK

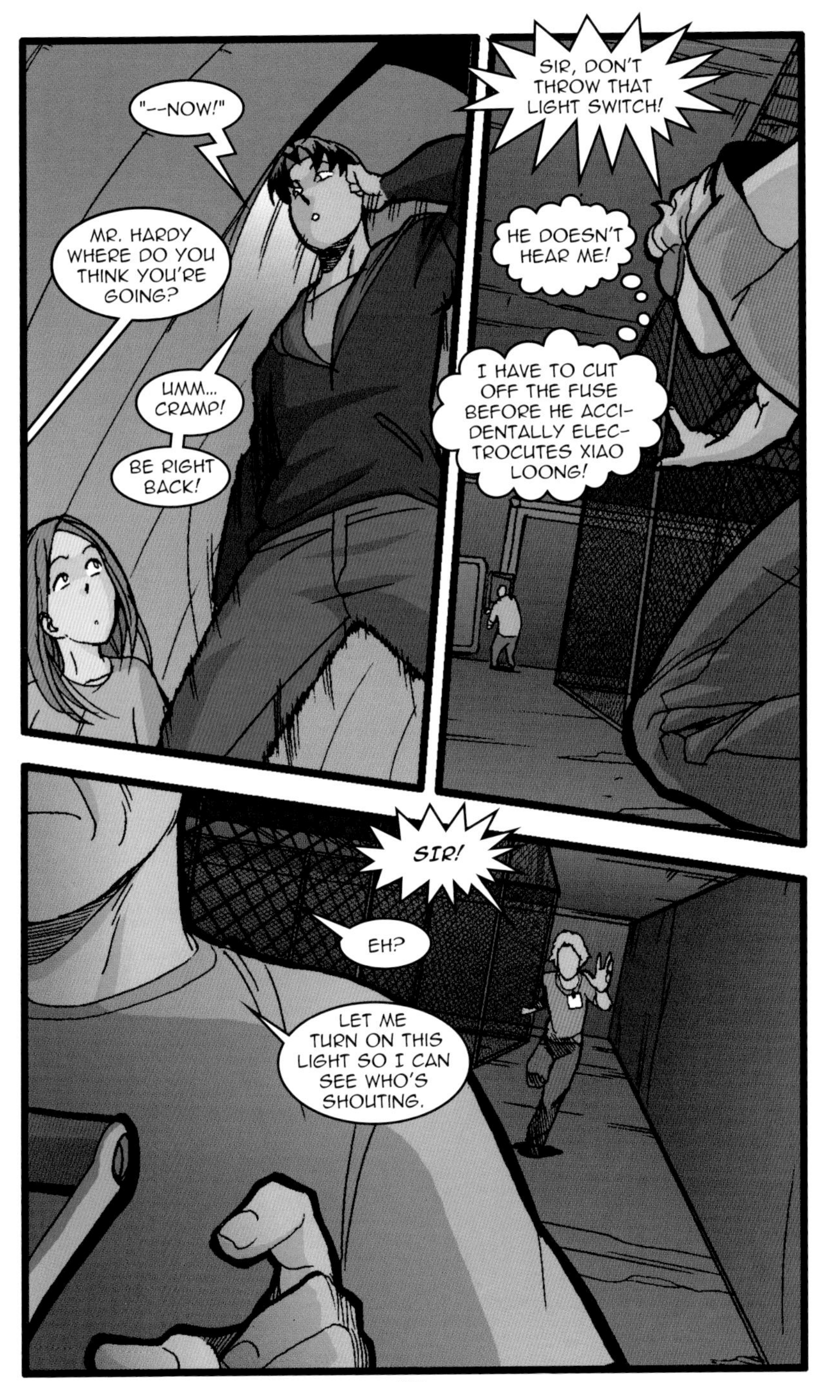
"--NOW!"
MR. HARDY WHERE DO YOU THINK YOU'RE GOING?
UMM... CRAMP!
BE RIGHT BACK!
SIR, DON'T THROW THAT LIGHT SWITCH!
HE DOESN'T HEAR ME!
I HAVE TO CUT OFF THE FUSE BEFORE HE ACCIDENTALLY ELECTROCUTES XIAO LOONG!
SIR!
EH?
LET ME TURN ON THIS LIGHT SO I CAN SEE WHO'S SHOUTING.

I THINK ITS MORE THAN BRIGHT ENOUGH IN HERE, DON'T YOU?
WHAT THE HECK--!
YOU SHOULDN'T BE BACK HERE-- YOU SCARED ME.

THAT WAS CLOSE!
FLIP

I DON'T SUPPOSE THERE'S ANY WAY YOU SAW WHO DID THIS TO YOU...?

I'M AFRAID NOT.
I WAS STRUCK FROM BEHIND.
I'M AFRAID I DIDN'T SEE HIDE NOR HAIR.

SPEAKING OF HAIR...
ANY CHANCE THIS SINGLE RED HAIR BELONGS TO YOUR ATTACKER?

ACTUALLY, NOW THAT I THINK ABOUT IT...
I HAVE THIS VAGUE MEMORY THAT WHEN I WOKE UP--
--I SAW A RED-HEADED GIRL RUNNING INTO THE SHADOWS.

I DON'T SEE HOW THAT IS HELPFUL.
THERE'RE NO REDHEADS IN THE COMPETITION.
IT COULD BE THE ASSAILANT WORE A WIG.
TO DISGUISE HERSELF. COULD THAT MEAN IT IS SOMEONE WE'D RECOGNIZE?

EXCUSE ME.
LUMLY, WHAT IS IT?
YOU MIGHT WANT TO SEE THIS.

LOVE IS AS LOVE IS.
LOVE ME ALL OR NOT AT ALL.
I DIDN'T KNOW SINGING WAS PART OF THIS CONTEST.
IT'S NOT, FARAH.
IT'S NOT.
OH, NO-- THAT CHANDE-LIER HAS COME LOOSE!
SHE'LL BE KILLED!
NO, SHE WON'T!
IF I CAN GET THERE IN TIME!

CHAPTER SEVEN:
"LIGHT OF THE WORLD!"
K-KRASH

THBUMP
HOW DID WE--?
AHNN!

THERE WAS A TRAP DOOR IN THE STAGE FLOOR!
GOOD THING OR WE WOULD HAVE BEEN CRUSHED!

LET'S LOOK FOR A WAY TO GET BACK UP THERE.
THE OTHERS MUST BE WOR-RIED ABOUT US.
NO DOUBT.

THAT'S WHY THIS ALL HAS TO END.
HERE.
NOW.
YOU...

...KNEW IT WAS ME ALL ALONG?
NO. BUT I FIGURED IT OUT.

ONLY A KILLER WITH A TREMENDOUS EGO WOULD RISK HER OWN LIFE TO GET ATTENTION.

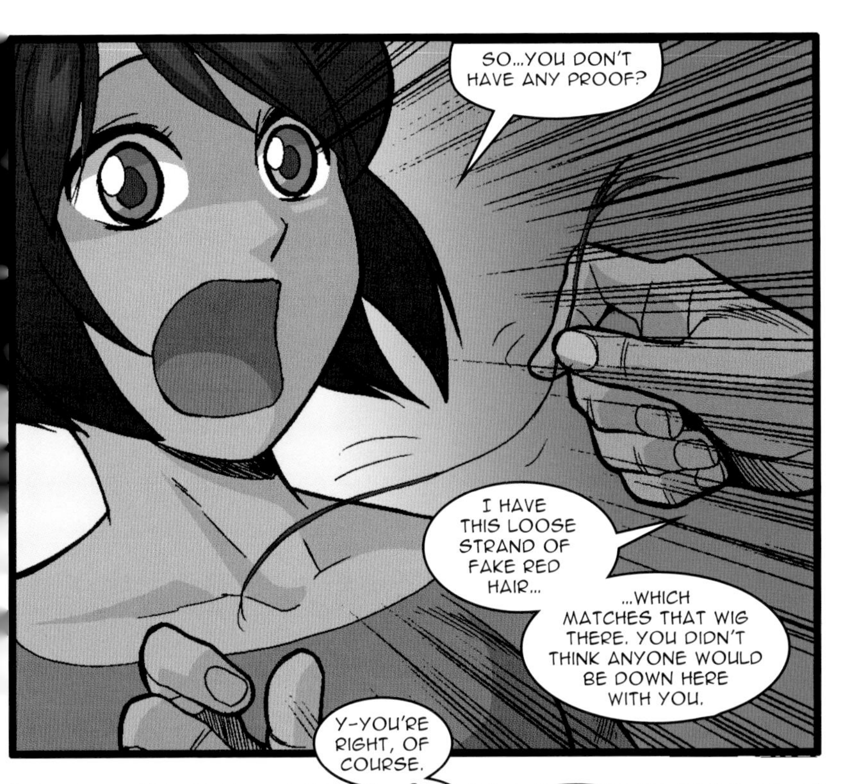
SO...YOU DON'T HAVE ANY PROOF?
I HAVE THIS LOOSE STRAND OF FAKE RED HAIR...
...WHICH MATCHES THAT WIG THERE. YOU DIDN'T THINK ANYONE WOULD BE DOWN HERE WITH YOU.

Y-YOU'RE RIGHT, OF COURSE.
I C-CAN'T DENY IT.

BUT...WHY?
WHAT WOULD POSSESS SOME-ONE LIKE ME TO DO SOMETHING LIKE THIS?

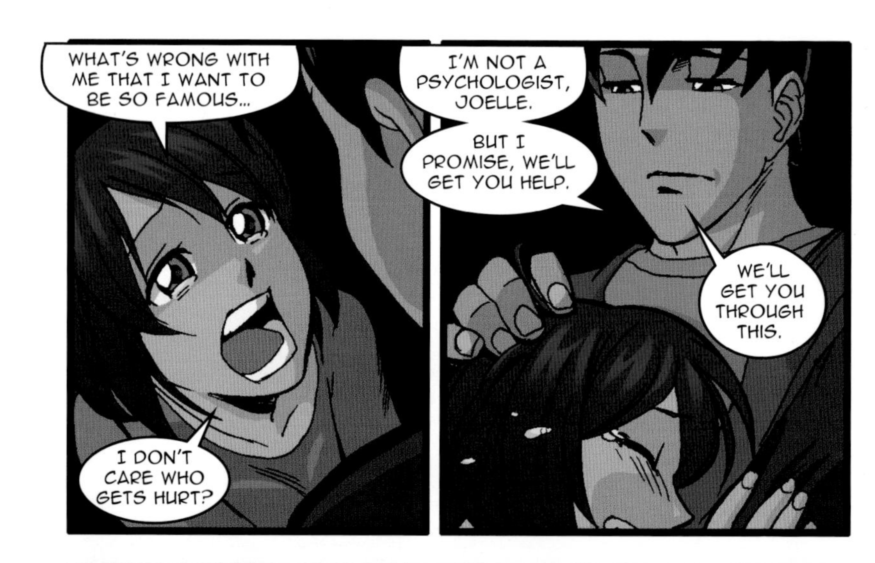
WHAT'S WRONG WITH ME THAT I WANT TO BE SO FAMOUS...
I DON'T CARE WHO GETS HURT?
I'M NOT A PSYCHOLOGIST, JOELLE.
BUT I PROMISE, WE'LL GET YOU HELP.
WE'LL GET YOU THROUGH THIS.

I KNEW THAT TRAP DOOR LED DOWN TO...
OH.

CHAPTER EIGHT:
"ENCORE!"
IF WE DON'T FIGHT FOR LOVE...
...THEN WE FIGHT FOR NOTHING AT ALL.

BRAVO!
CLAP
CLAP
CLAP
CLAP
BRAVO!
GO, FRANK!
CLAP
CLAP
CLAP
CLAP

CLAP
CLAP
CLAP
CLAP
CLAP
CLAP

CLAP
CLAP
CLAP

EVERYTHING IS GOING TO BE OKAY.
THOSE A.T.A.C. PSYCHOL-OGISTS ARE GOING TO HELP HER.
I KNOW.
THANKS.

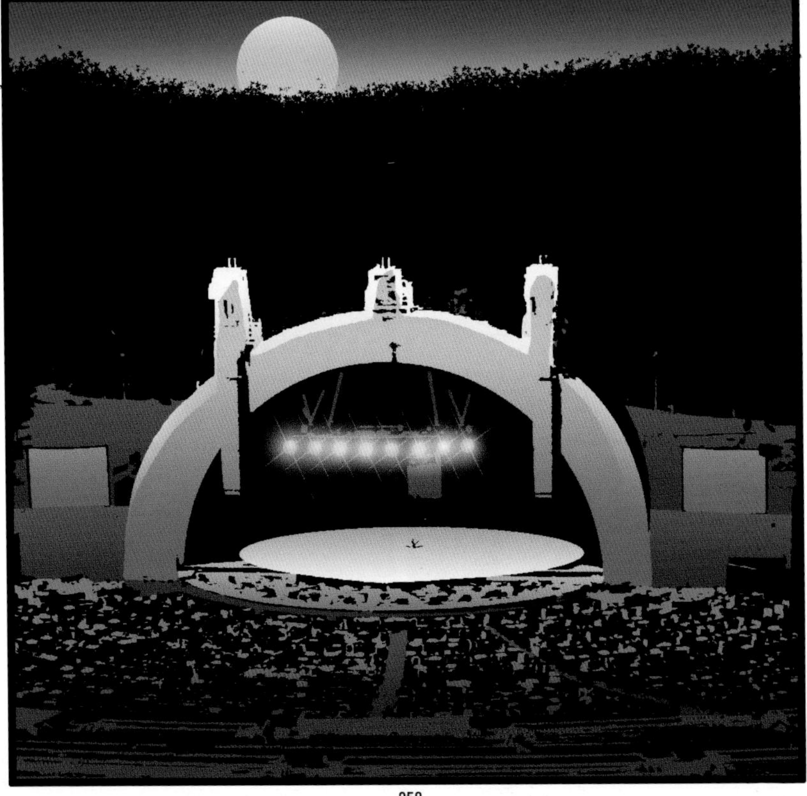

DIE, JOE HARDY!
DIE!
DIE
KIK
KIK
THANKS, NO. I'VE GOT OTHER PLANS FOR THIS WEEKEND.
THAT SOUNDED BRAVE ENOUGH...
"A HARDY DAY'S NIGHT"

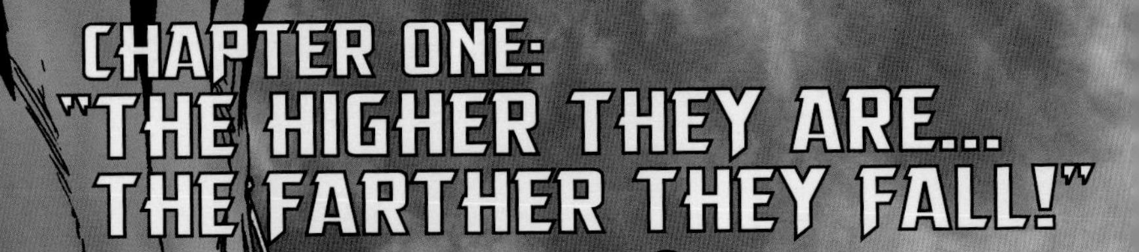
CHAPTER ONE:
"THE HIGHER THEY ARE... THE FARTHER THEY FALL!"
BUT IF THINGS DON'T TURN AROUND SOON...
...I'M GOING TO BE LITTLE MORE THAN A STAIN 10,000 FEET FROM NOW!
I'VE BEEN GETTING AWAY WITH MY CON FOR MONTHS.
YOU AND YOUR BROTHER HAVE COST ME THOUSANDS!
THAT'S NOT EVEN COUNTING THE LENGTHY PRISON TERM WHEN YOU'RE FINALLY CONVICTED.

MY KNIFE IS BRAND NEW. I GOT IT JUST FOR THIS CASE.
MAYBE THIS WILL MAKE UP FOR YOUR LOSSES?

HERE... CATCH!
WHA--?!
I HOPE THIS WORKS...
...IT'S A ONE IN A MILLION SHOT!

SLICE
PAH! YOUR AIM IS OFF BY--
--A MILE?!
IIIIEEEEE!
MAN, IS THIS GOING TO BE CLOSE!
REACH, SIR--REACH!
EH?!

ARE WE DONE WITH THE PART WHERE YOU TRY TO KILL ME?
Y-YES.
C-CAN WE GET TO THE P-PART--?
--WHERE YOU F-FIGURE OUT H-HOW WE'RE G-GOING TO GET D-DOWN SAFELY?

TRUST ME--
IT'S NOT GOING TO BE A PROBLEM!
THUPPA THUPPA THUPPA THUPPA
ISN'T THAT ALWAYS THE WAY IT IS, JOE?
I DO ALL THE RESCUING, WHILE YOU DO ALL THE HANGING AROUND?
FBI
L-LESS COMEDY-- MORE R-RESCUE?

SOON, AT AN AIRSTRIP OUTSIDE OF DENVER, COLORADO...
GOOD JOB, HARDY BOYS.
THIS MOUNTAIN GUIDE HAS BEEN ABANDONING TEEN CLIMBERS UP THERE FOR MONTHS--
--AND THEN LEADING THE RESCUE EFFORTS IN ORDER TO COLLECT THE REWARDS.
WE COULDN'T HAVE BUSTED THIS CASE WITHOUT A.T.A.C*.'S SUPPORT.
IT'S AN HONOR, SIR. NOW IF YOU EXCUSE ME--
--I NEED TO TALK TO MY BROTHER ABOUT HIS HOT-DOGGING ON THE CLIFFS.
*A.T.A.C.: AMERICAN TEENS AGAINST CRIME.
HEY, FRANK-- IT WORKED, DIDN'T IT?

CHAPTER TWO:
"DANCE 'TIL YOU DROP!"
A WEEK LATER, JOE HARDY IS HOT DOGGING IN AN ENTIRELY DIFFERENT VENUE...
...THE DANCE FLOOR OF THE BAYPORT HIGH SCHOOL GYM.
GO, JOE!
BOY, YOU CAN DANCE!
AWWW. YOU GIRLS JUST MAKE ME LOOK GOOD!

THEY MAY SPEND THEIR FREE TIME WORKING FOR A SUPER SECRET SPY ORGANIZATION...

BAYPORT DANCE 'TIL YOU DON'T DANCE!
...BUT THEY'RE STILL TEENAGED BOYS FINDING THEIR WAY IN THE WORLD.

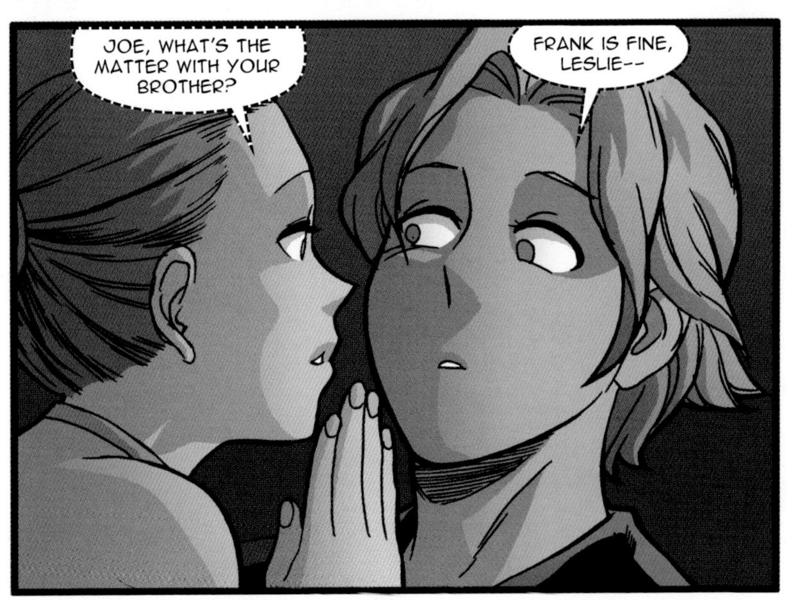
JOE, WHAT'S THE MATTER WITH YOUR BROTHER?
FRANK IS FINE, LESLIE--

"HE'S JUST A LITTLE SHY WHEN IT COMES TO GIRLS."
AND SO, IF YOU'RE NOT DOING ANY-THING...
...I WAS WONDERING IF YOU'D CARE TO JOIN ME ON THE DANCE FLOOR.

THAT SOUNDS A LITTLE FORMAL.
HMMM.
HOW ABOUT "HEY! WANNA' DANCE?!"
TOO INFORMAL?

YOU COULD ALWAYS JUST START DANCING AND SEE WHO BOOGIES UP NEXT TO YOU.
IT CERTAINLY SEEMS TO WORK FOR YOU.

I'M SORRY TO SAY I'M FEELING A LITTLE AWK-WARD.
JOELLE--THE LAST GIRL I WAS SERIOUS ABOUT--DIDN'T WORK OUT SO WELL.

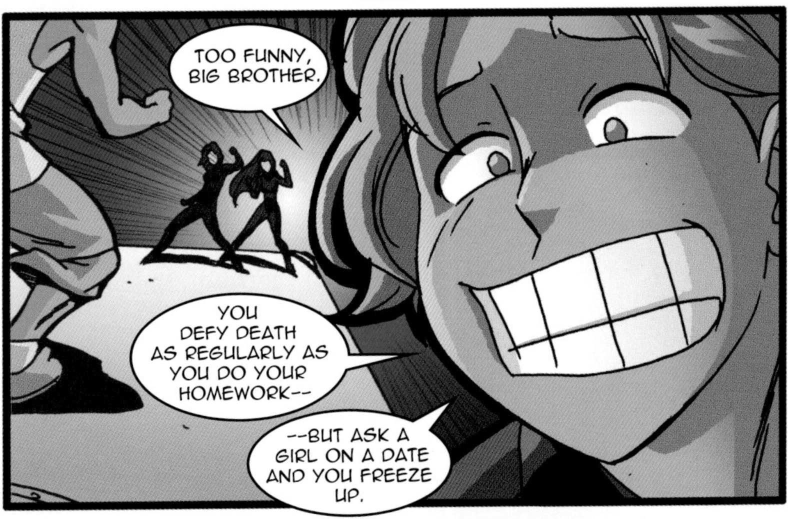
TOO FUNNY, BIG BROTHER.
YOU DEFY DEATH AS REGULARLY AS YOU DO YOUR HOMEWORK--
--BUT ASK A GIRL ON A DATE AND YOU FREEZE UP.

THAT'S HARDLY AN ACCURATE DE-SCRIPTION OF--
WHERE ARE WE GOING?
TO THAT HOTTIE YOU'VE BEEN EYEING ALL NIGHT!

EXCUSE ME, WOULD YOU LIKE TO DANCE?!
WHAT??
DID YOU SAY SOME-THING?
UM.

I WAS WONDERING IF YOU'D CARE TO JOIN ME.
ON THE DANCE FLOOR.
UM, DANCING.
GIGGLE

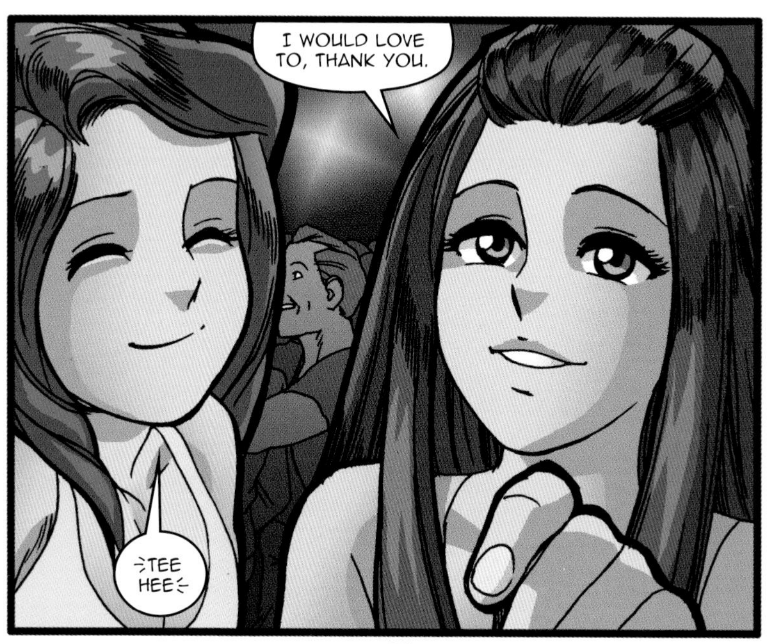
I WOULD LOVE TO, THANK YOU.
TEE HEE

SORRY--FRANK CAN'T DANCE JUST THIS SECOND!
MAYBE LATER?!
JOE--??

SAY "GOOD-BYE!"
SORRY?
HMP
WHY ARE THE CUTE ONES ALWAYS SO ODD?

WOULD YOU CARE TO EXPLAIN WHAT THAT WAS ALL ABOUT?
SORRY, FRANK-- SOMETHING CAME UP.
LOOK!

I JUST SPOTTED THIS GAME PACKAGE THAT WAS LEFT FOR US ON THIS CHAIR.
AND YOU KNOW WHAT THAT MEANS.
FIFTY YARD LINE
IT'S HOW A.T.A.C. PROVIDES US WITH DETAILS FOR OUR NEXT CASE.

WHICH IS WHY IT'S SO DISCON-CERTING TO FIND THIS CASE...

...IS EMPTY!
WHAT-- HOW IS THAT POSSIBLE?

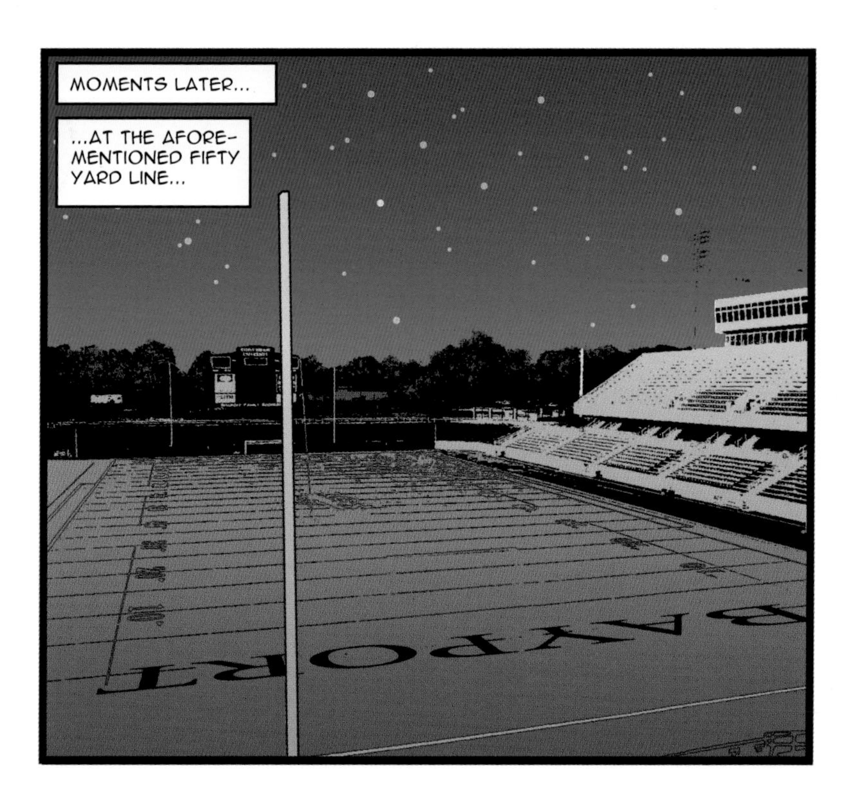
MOMENTS LATER...
...AT THE AFORE-MENTIONED FIFTY YARD LINE...
BAYPORT

THIS SEEMS AS LIKELY A PLACE AS ANY TO FIGURE OUT WHAT HAPPENED TO THE GAME DISC.
IT IS THE NEAREST FIFTY YARD LINE.

DID A.T.A.C. LEAVE US AN EMPTY BOX AS A CLUE--
--OR DID SOMEONE STEAL THE DISC?

HMM. THE ONLY THING DIFFERENT BETWEEN THE BOX AND THIS PARTICULAR SPOT IS...
1

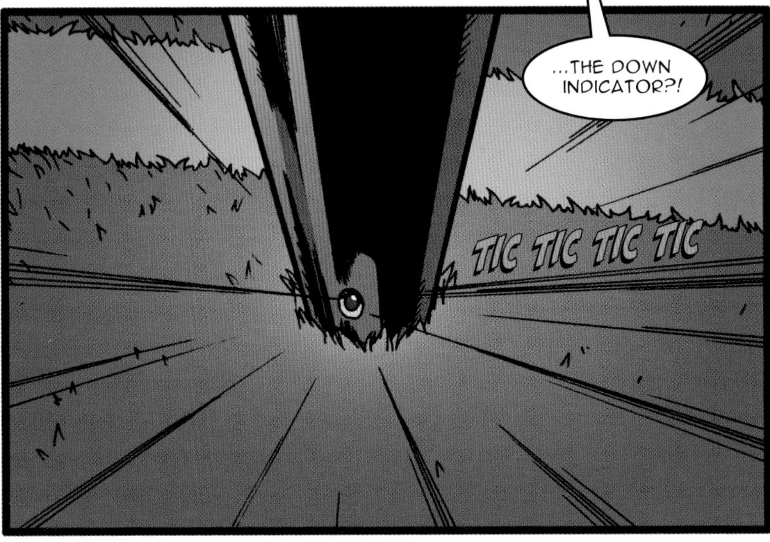
...THE DOWN INDICATOR?!
TIC TIC TIC TIC

CHAPTER THREE:
"OUT OF BOUNDS!"
BARRA-BA-
BOOM

JOE...YOU OKAY?
BECAUSE YOU SPOTTED THAT BOMB, I AM.
ANOTHER SECOND AND WE'D HAVE BEEN TOAST!
WHO COULD HAVE--
SHHHH
I CAN HEAR SOMEONE COMING!

OH, NO--
WHAT HAVE I
DONE?
WHAT HAVE
I DONE?
FUNNY, WE
WERE WONDERING
THE SAME THING!
WHA--?!
WHAMP

MAYBE HIS IDENTITY WILL SHINE SOME LIGHT ON HIS MOTIVES!
THEN AGAIN--
--MAYBE NOT?
YOU! BUT...WHY?

YOU'RE CARL BRUCKNER--ONE OF DAD'S CLOSEST FRIENDS!
THIS DOESN'T MAKE ANY SENSE.

I CAN REMEMBER YOU AND DAD WORKING AT THE KITCHEN TABLE--
--TRYING TO SOLVE CASES NO MATTER HOW LONG THEY TOOK.
YOU WERE THERE THE FIRST DAY WE CAME TO A.T.A.C. HEADQUARTERS.
DAD'S ALWAYS TRUSTED YOU-- WE ALL HAVE.
I-I'VE ALWAYS THOUGHT OF THE TWO OF YOU AS SONS--
--YOU WERE EVEN THERE AT MY MICKEY'S BIRTHDAY PARTY LAST MONTH.

THIS DOESN'T MAKE ANY SENSE.
WHY WOULD YOU WANT TO KILL US WITH A BOMB?

MICKEY'S BEEN KIDNAPPED!
THE ONLY WAY I COULD BUY HIS LIFE... WAS WITH YOURS!

I GOT HOME YESTERDAY TO LEARN MY ONLY SON HAD BEEN ABDUCTED.
MY WIFE HANDED ME THE RANSOM NOTE.

"THE INSTRUCTIONS WERE CLEAR. IF I DISOBEYED THEM, MICKEY WOULD BE KILLED.
"I WAS ORDERED TO MEET A MAN IN AN ALLEY--
"--HE GAVE ME THE DETAILS."

"IF MICKEY IS TO LIVE-- I HAVE TO PROVIDE HIM WITH PROOF THAT YOU TWO ARE DEAD."

YOU HAVE TO UNDERSTAND...
...I'D DO ANYTHING TO SAVE MY SON.
ANYTHING.

THERE'S ONLY ONE THING WE CAN DO AT THIS POINT...
I'LL SAY. I'LL GO CALL THE--

IF WE'RE GOING TO HELP...
...WE HAVE TO DIE.
?!

FRANK?
MR.BRUCKNER'S HEART WASN'T IN THAT BOMB.
IT WAS MORE SMOKE THAN EXPLOSION. IF HE WANTED TO KILL US--
I HEAR WHAT YOU'RE SAYING, FRANK.
BUT THAT DOESN'T MEAN I HAVE TO BE EXCITED ABOUT HELPING HIM.
WE'RE NOT, NECESSARILY...
...WE'RE ALL HELPING MICKEY--TOGETHER!
NOW WE HAVE TO MOVE QUICKLY BEFORE THE SMOKE DISSIPATES!

TEN MINUTES LATER...
CHAPTER FOUR:
"I CHARGE YOU WITH THE MURDER OF THE HARDY BOYS!"

WEEOO WEEOO WEEOO

click
click

DOWNSTAIRS...
MORGUE
THIS MIGHT BE EASIER IF WE KNEW WHO IT WAS THAT WANTS US SO DEAD.
WELL, EVER SINCE WE STARTED WORKING FOR DAD AND A.T.A.C...
...WE'VE CERTAINLY MADE OUR SHARE OF ENEMIES.
BEING ARRESTED WILL DO THAT TO A PERSON.
IT'S DEFINITELY SOMEONE WITH A LOT OF RESOURCES IF HE WAS ABLE TO KIDNAP THE SON OF AN A.T.A.C. MENTOR AGENT.

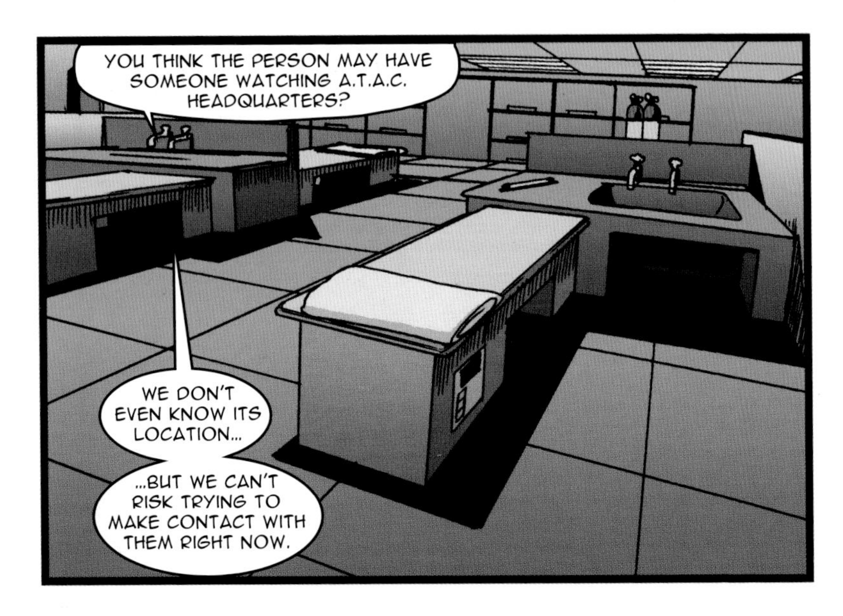
YOU THINK THE PERSON MAY HAVE SOMEONE WATCHING A.T.A.C. HEADQUARTERS?
WE DON'T EVEN KNOW ITS LOCATION...
...BUT WE CAN'T RISK TRYING TO MAKE CONTACT WITH THEM RIGHT NOW.

SO WE'RE GOING TO MAKE DUE WITH THE RESOURCES WE HAVE.
IS THAT... AN ULTRA-VIOLET SCANNER?

GOOD CALL. YES, AND BY ILLUMINATING SPECIAL DE-TAILS ALONG THE LIGHT SPECTRUM...

YOU'RE GOING ALL SCIENCE GEEK ON ME, FRANK.
CAN WE CUT TO THE CLUE?
RIGHT. THERE'S ONE THERE...
Saint John's Hotel
A WATERMARK ON THE STATIONERY.
NOW WE KNOW WHERE THE PAPER CAME FROM.

GREAT. NOW WE JUST HAVE TO GET THERE, FIND THE KID AND FREE HIM.
WHAT COULD POSSIBLY GO WRONG?

CHAPTER FIVE: "LESS IS MORGUE!"
YOU MEAN BESIDES THIS MOOSE OF A MAN TRYING TO SNEAK UP ON US?
A NINJA HE'S NOT.
WE HEARD HIM FROM OUT IN THE HALLWAY.

THIS IS ONE LOW GRADE ASSASSIN, I HAVE TO SAY.
WHAM
WE CAN'T QUESTION HIM IF HE'S OUT COLD.
OUR BIGGER PROBLEM IS WHAT DO WE DO WITH HIM--
--SO HE DOESN'T CONTACT HIS BOSS WHEN HE'S CON-SCIOUS.

SEVERAL ROLLS OF DUCT TAPE LATER...
THAT OUGHT TO DO IT.

NOW, LET'S GO! SAINT JOHN'S HOTEL IS DOWN-TOWN...
...IT SHOULDN'T TAKE US FIFTEEN MINUTES TO GET THERE!

"OF COURSE GETTING IN--
"--THAT MIGHT BE A PROBLEM."
I HATE TO THINK OF MICKEY TRAPPED INSIDE THAT DUMP.

IT LOOKS LIKE NO ONE HAS BEEN THERE FOR YEARS.

IN THE 1920S, IT WAS ONE OF THE COUNTRY'S MOST POPULAR HOTELS.
THE RICH AND FAMOUS FROM AROUND THE WORLD WOULD STAY THERE.

"IT WAS A PLACE WHERE YOU COULD DANCE AND DRINK ALL NIGHT."

BUT...THAT WAS DURING PROHIBITION, WHEN ALCOHOL WAS ILLEGAL.

"YES, JOE--THE OWNERS USED TO HAVE TO SMUGGLE LIQUOR IN THROUGH CLANDESTINE TUNNELS."

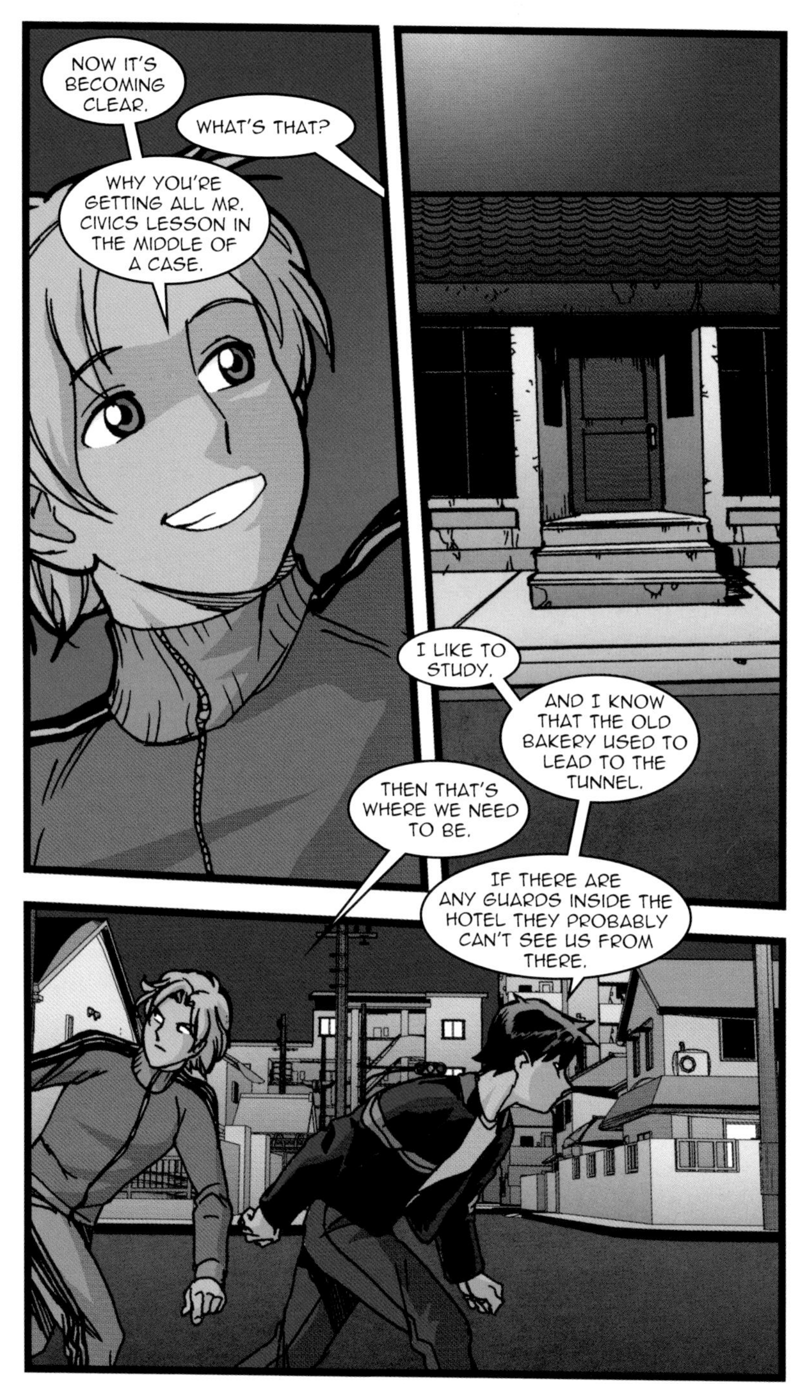
NOW IT'S BECOMING CLEAR.
WHAT'S THAT?
WHY YOU'RE GETTING ALL MR. CIVICS LESSON IN THE MIDDLE OF A CASE.
I LIKE TO STUDY.
AND I KNOW THAT THE OLD BAKERY USED TO LEAD TO THE TUNNEL.
THEN THAT'S WHERE WE NEED TO BE.
IF THERE ARE ANY GUARDS INSIDE THE HOTEL THEY PROBABLY CAN'T SEE US FROM THERE.

NOBODY HAS BEEN IN HERE FOR YEARS.
I DON'T SUPPOSE YOUR TEXT BOOK TOLD YOU WHERE THE SECRET ENTRANCE MIGHT BE?
NO, BUT I'M GUESSING SINCE THE TUNNELS ARE UNDERGROUND--
--THE ENTRANCE MIGHT BE POINTING DOWN.
I SHOULD HAVE FIGURED THAT ONE OUT ON MY OWN.

THERE ARE NO FOOT-PRINTS ON THE FLOOR. NO COBWEBS HAVE BEEN DISPLACED.
IF MICKEY IS IN THE HOTEL, IT'S UNLIKELY ANY OF THE KIDNAPPERS CAME THROUGH HERE.
THAT MEANS WE MIGHT HAVE THE ADVANTAGE OF SURPRISE.

LET'S HOPE SO. POOR KID.

THIS PLACE IS THE DUMPS. EVEN RATS DON'T WANT TO BE HERE.
SKWEE!

IT WAS ONCE A GRAND AND GLAMOROUS PLACE.
BUT THAT WAS A VERY LONG TIME AGO.
CLEARLY.
IF THAT'S NOT ABANDONED...
IT'S JUST THE LOBBY, JOE. THERE COULD BE PEOPLE ON THE UPPER FLOORS.
THEN I GUESS I NEED TO TAKE A CLOSER LOOK.
YOU STAY HERE

NOT ANOTHER MOVE, PUNK.
WHAT ARE YOU DOING HERE?
CH-CHAK
MY FRIEND DARED ME TO WALK DOWN A TUNNEL!
PLEASE, MISTER--I DON'T EVEN KNOW WHERE I AM!

SORRY, KID. THIS IS YOUR UNLUCKY DAY.
GET MOVING, AND DON'T TRY ANYTHING.
S-SURE, MISTER. CAN YOU DO M-ME A FAVOR?
WHAT'S THAT, KID?
WATCH WHERE YOU'RE GOING!
WHA -- ?!

GOOD ADVICE, JOE!

WHAM
UHN!

WHERE'S MY--
--MY GUN!?

DON'T WORRY, I'VE GOT IT.
AND UNLIKE YOU, I'M POLITE ENOUGH TO POINT IT AWAY FROM ANYONE.

I'M GOIN' TO BE...IN SO MUCH...
BONK
AT LEAST NOW WE KNOW THERE ARE ARMED GUARDS AROUND.
OF COURSE THIS GUN IS NO USE IF I TAKE OUT THE AMMO.
I'LL SCOUT AHEAD.

IF THIS WERE AN A.T.A.C. CASE, THEY MIGHT HAVE PROVIDED US WITH GADGETS.
AS IT IS, IT'S JUST THE TWO OF US AGAINST WHO KNOWS WHAT?

THIS ELEVATOR LEADS UPSTAIRS. BUT WITH NO POWER IN THE BUILDING...
IT'S USELESS.
NOT NECESSARILY.

GRAB A DOOR...
...AND PULL.
PULLING.

CAN YOU SEE ANYTHING?
JUST THE TOP OF THE CAR.

THERE'S LIGHT COMING FROM UP ABOVE.
THEY MUST HAVE WIRED THE BUILDING IN ORDER TO POWER THE TOP FLOORS.

CHANCES ARE, THAT'S WHERE THEY'RE KEEPING MICKEY.
AND CHANCES ARE EVEN GREATER--THEY HAVE GUARDS IN THE STAIRWELL.

SOON...
IT'S A GOOD THING WE STAY IN SHAPE AND EXERCISE...
...OR WE COULD NEVER PULL THIS OFF.
IT'S A LOT HARDER THAN IT LOOKS!
LET'S HOPE FOR MICKEY'S SAKE WE'VE GOTTEN HERE IN TIME.
HE'LL BE FINE, FRANK--I'M SURE OF IT.

NOW, SHUSH...
...UNTIL WE GET ABOVE THE FLOOR THAT'S LIT UP.

NOW WE CAN LOOK DOWN ON THEM AND GET A LAY OF THE LAND.

THERE'S A RAILING UP AHEAD. WE CAN SPY ON THEM WITHOUT ANYONE SEEING US.

IT LOOKS LIKE...A BALCONY.
DO YOU THINK WE'RE OVERLOOK-ING A STAGE?

SOMETHING LIKE THAT. BUT MORE LIKE...

THAT IS ONE WELL-GUARDED HOSTAGE.
DO YOU HAVE A PLAN?
NOT YET, NO.

HMMM.
TOUGH ONE.
WHAT IF...

NOW THAT WE KNOW WHERE HE IS, WE CALL THE POLICE.
THAT WOULD BE PERFECT, BUT--
--TIME IS OF THE ESSENCE. IF THAT ASSASSIN FROM THE HOSPITAL REPORTS WE'RE STILL ALIVE...?
THAT WOULD BE BAD FOR MICKEY.
THIS IS GOING TO SOUND CRAZY BUT...

SQUEESQUEESQUEESQUEE
HUNH?

WHAT'S THAT NOISE?

SQUEESQUEESQUEESQUEE

LOOK WHAT WE GOT HERE-- A RUNAWAY ROOM SERVICE CART. DINNER IS SERVED...
WOULDN'T IT BE ROTTEN BY NOW?
SQUEE...

NOPE. NOTHING.
TOO BAD. I'M STARVING.

JUST AS WELL... I'VE HEARD THIS WHOLE HOTEL IS HAUNTED.
S-SERIOUS?
?!

ENOUGH WITH THAT NONSENSE TALK! THERE'S NO SUCH THING...

NOT VERY.
TH-THAT'S GOOD TO KNOW.
... AS GHOSTS?

WHAT'S GOING ON?!
RELAX, IT'S ONLY FAULTY WIRING.
THIS BUILDING IS NEARLY ONE HUN-DRED YEARS OLD, REMEMBER?

THERE'S ABSOLUTELY NOTHING TO...
RATTLE
RATTLE
RATTLE
...WORRY... ABOUT.

NOTHING TO FEAR BUT ME, FRANK HARDY-- "GHOST."

THIS IS RIDICULOUS!
GHOSTS AREN'T REAL!
KICK

LOOK! THE BOY--HE'S GONE!

WE'VE BEEN SET UP! AIM...AND FIRE ON MY COMMAND!
READY...
...AIM...

CHAPTER SIX:
"BRINGING DOWN THE HOUSE!"
CRASH
THERE IS A GHOST-- I KNEW IT!
HOW DID--?!
IIIIIIIEEEE!

THAT WAS CLOSER THAN I WANTED IT TO BE!
BUT IT WILL KEEP THEM PINNED DOWN WHILE I RENDEZVOUS WITH JOE.
WITH THE GUARDS TRAPPED, THE STAIRWELL SHOULD GET ME DOWN TO THE LOBBY IN NO TIME.

MEANWHILE...
ISN'T THIS FUN, MICKEY? KEEP AN EYE OUT FOR FRANK.
THIS IS A GREAT GAME, JOE!
BETTER HE THINKS WE'RE PLAYING TAG THAN ESCAPING FROM WOULD-BE KILLERS!

HEY, GUYS--
DID I MISS
ANYTHING?
HA HA!
YOU'RE IT!
THAT'S FRANK,
ALWAYS IT WHEN
YOU NEED HIM.
WHY DON'T
WE TAKE THIS
GAME OUT-
SIDE?
WEEE!
THERE'S
MORE ROOM
TO RUN AROUND!

TUT TUT.
LEAVING THE
HOTEL, HARDY
BOYS?
THAT WOULD
BE CHEATING.

NO WAY WE'RE GETTING PAST THIS GUY.
NEW GAME, MICKEY. CLOSE YOUR EYES AND COUNT TO ONE HUNDRED.
ONE...TWO...
TO YOURSELF.
I HAVE LOOKED FORWARD TO THE DAY I COULD AVENGE MY FAMILY.
UM, DO WE KNOW THIS GUY?
I'M SURE WE'VE NEVER MET HIM.

CORRECT, FRANK. YOU HAVE NOT
BUT YOU DID MEET MY DAUGHTERS, SHIRA AND NICOLINA. I AM POPPA NOIR.
IF I HAD NOT FREED THEM, YOUR ACTIONS WOULD HAVE CAUSED THEIR ARREST.
IN OUR DEFENSE, SIR THEY WERE TRYING TO KILL US.
APPARENTLY ALL YOU NOIRS ARE A LITTLE BLOOD-THIRSTY.

WE GOT HERE AS QUICKLY AS WE COULD, SIR.
NOW WE HAVE THEM SURROUNDED.

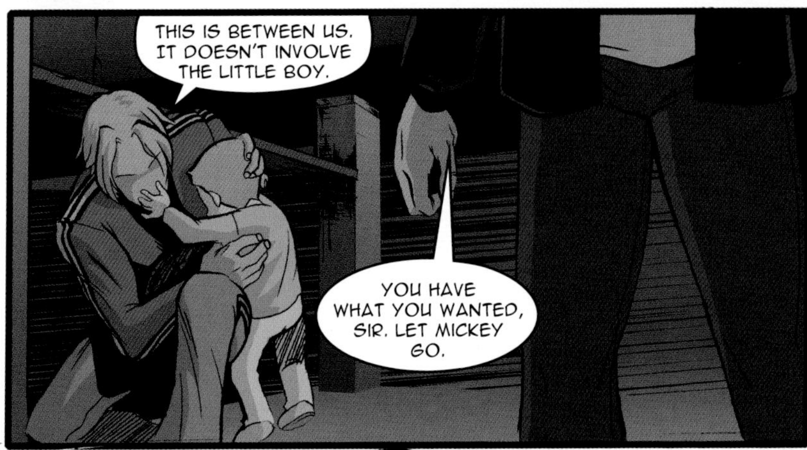
THIS IS BETWEEN US. IT DOESN'T INVOLVE THE LITTLE BOY.
YOU HAVE WHAT YOU WANTED, SIR. LET MICKEY GO.

ARE YOU... ARE YOU SERIOUS? YOUR ONLY CONCERN NOW IS FOR THE CHILD?
THE GIRLS SAID YOU TWO WERE QUITE... UNIQUE.

CHALK IT UP TO GOOD GENES, NOIR.

DAD?!

AS I LIVE AND BREATHE-- IT'S FENTON HARDY, THE FOUNDER OF A.T.A.C..
THIS IS A MUCH BIGGER CATCH THAN THE HARDY BOYS.

HELLO, BOYS. WHEN CARL WAS BROUGHT INTO CUSTODY HE TOLD ME WHAT HAPPENED.
I'VE BEEN A FEW STEPS BEHIND YOU.
UNTIL NOW.

NOIR, TAKE ME. FATHER TO FATHER.
THERE'S NO REASON TO INVOLVE OUR CHILDREN IN ALL OF THIS.
DAD, NO!
WE WON'T LET YOU DO THIS.
YOU DON'T GET A VOTE, BOYS.
WHAT DO YOU SAY, NOIR?

FINE.
AWAY, HARDY BOYS. AND TAKE THE CHILD WITH YOU.

UM, EXCUSE ME.
THEY'RE JUST GOING TO GO TO THE POLICE!

LET THEM.
WE'LL BE LONG GONE BY THE TIME THE AUTHORITIES ARRIVE.
CR-CLAK

DAD?
THERE'S GOT TO BE ANOTHER WAY.
GO. NOW.
THAT'S AN ORDER.

YOU TWO GUARDS, BRING THE VAN AROUND TO THE ALLEY OUT BACK.
I'D LIKE TO TALK TO MR. HARDY ALONE A MOMENT.

SO TELL ME, FENTON--HOW DOES IT FEEL?
KNOWING THAT I'M GOING TO EXTRACT ALL OF A.T.A.C.'S SECRETS FROM YOU?

HONESTLY?
I FEEL TERRIBLY SAD FOR YOU.

?!
I KNOW WHAT IT'S LIKE TO BE A FATHER. TO HAVE GIVEN LIFE.
YOU WERE BLESSED WITH TWO LOVELY AND INNOCENT DAUGHTERS.

AND HOW DID YOU HONOR THE FAITH THEY PUT IN THEIR FATHER?
BY GROOMING THEM TO BE KILLERS.
YOU ARE GOING TO HAVE TO LIVE WITH THAT THE REST OF YOUR LIFE.

ENOUGH!
I WILL NOT BE LECTURED TO A MOMENT LONGER!

NOW COME ALONG, MR. "FATHER OF THE YEAR."
TELLING ME HOW TO RAISE MY DAUGHTERS? WHAT NERVE.

WHAT ABOUT YOU? YOU ENLISTED YOUR OWN SONS IN A.T.A.C..

THEY'RE UNDERCOVER SPIES, NOT KILLERS.
THEY HELP OTHER TEENS, THEY DON'T HURT.

DRIVER, TAKE US AWAY FROM HERE!

MY WIFE DIED NEARLY FIFTEEN YEARS AGO.
YOU DON'T KNOW WHAT IT'S LIKE, TRYING TO RAISE TWO DAUGHTERS WITHOUT A MOTHER.
I KNOW A FATHER'S LOVE IS A VERY POWERFUL THING.
WHAT ARE YOU SAYING--I DON'T LOVE MY DAUGHTERS ENOUGH TO DO THE RIGHT THING?!
WHAP
SOMETHING LIKE THAT, YES.

DID THIS VAN STOP MOVING?

YES...IT DID. WE MUST HAVE ARRIVED AT OUR DESTINATION.
GET OUT.

HERE WE ARE. NOT THE CLEANEST PLACE TO DIE, EH?
"DIE"? I THOUGHT YOU WANTED INFOR-MATION.

CHAPTER SEVEN:
"THE FINAL TARGET!"
I DID. UNTIL YOU STARTED TALKING SMACK ABOUT MY SKILLS AS A DAD.
NOW I JUST WANT TO SEE YOU DEAD.

PUT DOWN YOUR WEAPON, NOW!
EH?!
I REPEAT: PUT DOWN YOUR WEAPON! YOU ARE UNDER ARREST.
H-HOW IS THIS POSSIBLE? WHAT DID YOU DO, HARDY?
I'M AS SURPRISED AS YOU ARE. I CAN'T TAKE ANY CREDIT FOR THIS.

DAD, YOU'RE SAFE!
YOUR PLAN WORKED PERFECTLY, FRANK...

"... AFTER WE OVERPOWERED THE GUARDS..."
"... YOU DROVE WHILE I NOTIFIED THE POLICE ON THE TRUCK'S TWO WAY RADIO."

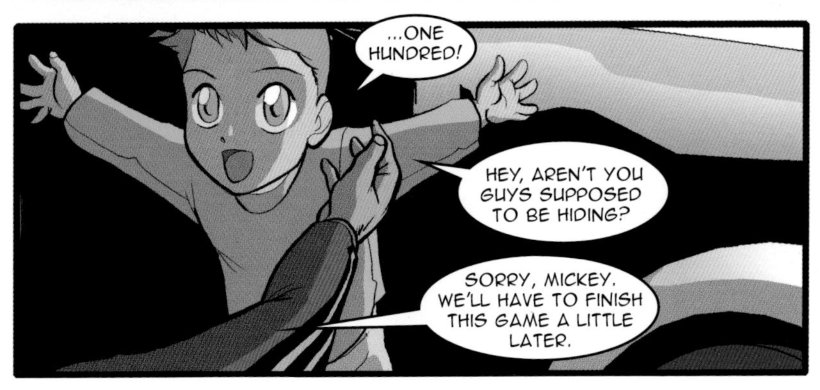
...ONE HUNDRED!
HEY, AREN'T YOU GUYS SUPPOSED TO BE HIDING?
SORRY, MICKEY. WE'LL HAVE TO FINISH THIS GAME A LITTLE LATER.

THANK YOU FOR YOUR TIMELY ASSISTANCE, SHERIFF COLLIG.
I'M ONLY GLAD WE COULD BACK UP YOUR SONS' PLAN.

NONE OF US BELIEVE WE'VE SEEN THE LAST OF HIM YET, DO WE?
I DIDN'T THINK SO.

DADDY!
MR. BRUCKNER, HERE? DAD...?
HE HELPED TRACK YOU DOWN. KEEPING HIM INVOLVED WAS THE LEAST I COULD DO.

CHAPTER EIGHT:
"FATHER AND SONS"

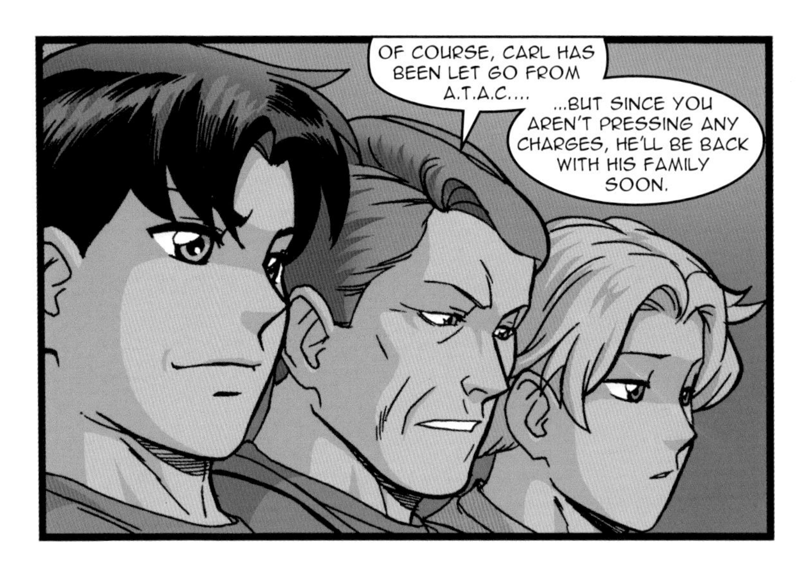
OF COURSE, CARL HAS BEEN LET GO FROM A.T.A.C....
...BUT SINCE YOU AREN'T PRESSING ANY CHARGES, HE'LL BE BACK WITH HIS FAMILY SOON.

WE HONESTLY DON'T BELIEVE HE TRIED TO KILL US.
OTHERWISE HE WOULD HAVE USED A DEADLIER BOMB. AND DAD...

... YOU SHOWED US FIRST HAND WHAT A FATHER WOULD RISK TO SAVE HIS SON. OR SONS.

HEY! MY LINE!
YOU GOT A BITE!

I'LL GET THE NET!
I'VE GOT HIM! I'VE GOT HIM! I'VE GOT--

SNAP
--NOTHING?

THAT ROTS BIG TIME.
MAYBE NOT. MAYBE THE FISH GETS TO GO HOME TO HIS FATHER, OR SON, OR BROTHER.

WHAT DO YOU THINK, DAD?
I THINK I AM THE LUCKIEST FATHER IN THE WORLD.

AND THAT I LOVE YOU BOTH WITH ALL MY HEART.
ME TOO, DAD.
AND ME THREE.

OKAY. NOW LET'S DO SOME FISHING!
RIGHT! THE WOMEN FOLK ARE COUNTING ON US.
"WOMEN FOLK"? YOU'RE SUCH A GOOFBALL.

WAS I A GOOFBALL WHEN I SAVED YOU FROM THAT--
BOYS? LESS TALKING. MORE FISHING.

HEY! I'VE GOT SOMETHING!
REEL HER IN!
I HAVE THE NET!
THE END

WATCH OUT FOR PAPERCUTZ™

Hi, mystery-lovers! Welcome to the first, fast-paced, fear-fraught HARDY BOYS ADVENTURES graphic novel by Scott Lobdell, writer, and PH Marcondes, Daniel Rendon, and Sidney Lima, artists, from Papercutz—those bright-day detectives dedicated to publishing great graphic novels for all ages. I'm Jim Salicrup, the Editor-in-Chief and part-time cleaner of Playback's birdcage.

If you're unfamiliar with Papercutz, may I suggest taking a quick look at our website, papercutz.com, and check out the wide range of graphic novels that we proudly publish. Let me warn you though, you may find a whole bunch of cool graphic novels that you'll want to get your hands on. Which is exactly why Papercutz was created—to provide compelling graphic novels to people such as you.

It all began back in 2005, when the first two Papercutz graphic novels were originally published – NANCY DREW GIRL DETECTIVE and THE HARDY BOYS UNDERCOVER BROTHERS. These were all-new comics starring the famed teen sleuths in adventures inspired by their then-current Simon and Schuster series. Now, over ten years later we've decided to bring back into print some of those action-packed adventures for a new generation to enjoy. We've already had success repackaging the NANCY DREW graphic novels, offering two-graphic-novels-in-one in our NANCY DREW DIARIES series, so it seemed the time was right to offer four-graphic-novels-in-one with HARDY BOYS ADVENTURES. That's right, we're packing four complete classic adventures into each volume of this new series. (No need to thank us!)

Inspired by Franklin W. Dixon's novels, Scott Lobdell has taken the Undercover Brothers to some interesting places. In this volume we see Frank and Joe battling the naughty Noir Sisters atop the speeding Silverado bullet train on its way to California, where Frank prepares to make his acting debut at the famed Hollywood Bowl, and Joe takes part in an extreme skate-boarding competition. You may think Frank and Joe get their orders from A.T.A.C.'s Nigel Penhurst, but it's really writer Scott Lobdell who keeps assigning the boys their missions. Scott an awesome comics writer, who has written every top comicbook series there is, from Marvel's X-MEN to DC Comics' SUPERMAN, as well as creating many original series himself. He has also done stand-up comedy, written movies and TV shows, and been a great friend of mine for many years. We're excited to be bringing these comics back into print at long last.

As for the artwork, well, let me tell you about the Boys from Brazil...

In this crazy world, who would've ever thought that such All-American icons such as the Hardy Boys would ever get a Manga-makeover and appear in graphic novels? The reasoning, by Papercutz publisher Terry Nantier, was that back in 2005, manga was all the rage in bookstores all across North America. Terry thought if fans were enjoying the somewhat strange comics coming from a very different culture than ours, maybe an even wider audience would enjoy a more traditionally American style of story illustrated in a manga-like style. The idea certainly went over well with booksellers, as both series launched very successfully into the market. And the fans loved it too!

PH

But as the editor of these graphic novels I had to ask myself, where would we find such artists? For NANCY DREW, the answer was finding Sho Murase, an animator who is half Korean, half Japanese, and who grew up in Spain (Spanish is her first language) and lives in San Francisco. For HARDY BOYS it took awhile until we found PH MARCONDES, or as he called himself back then, Paulo Henrique. In "The Opposite Numbers," PH was called in, along with our then-ZORRO artist Sidney Lima, to help departing HARDY BOYS artist Daniel Rendon complete that graphic novel. All three artists live in Brazil, which has a thriving comics creator community. PH's manga-inspired style is perhaps the manga-ist of the three. PH's style has, like manga, moments when it can be very humorous, but it's also a joyful style, bursting with excitement. PH not only went on to draw the majority of Papercutz HARDY BOYS graphic novels, but he also drew such hit series as LEGO® NINJAGO and SABAN'S POWER RANGERS. PH is currently drawing the latest, and perhaps greatest, Papercutz series—THE ZODIAC LEGACY.

Stan "the Man" Lee checks out THE ZODIAC LEGACY from Papercutz.

STAY IN TOUCH!

EMAIL: salicrup@papercutz.com
WEB: papercutz.com
TWITTER: @papercutzgn
FACEBOOK: PAPERCUTZGRAPHICNOVELS
FANMAIL: Papercutz, 160 Broadway, Suite 700, East Wing, New York, NY 10038

If you haven't read THE ZODIAC LEGACY best-selling novels by creator Stan Lee (Yes, that Stan Lee!) and writer Stuart Moore, do yourself a favor and get those books right now! Then you'll want to pick up the graphic novels, written by Stuart Moore and illustrated by PH Marcondes! The graphic novels aren't adaptations of the novels—they're all-new stories that fit together with the prose novels. To get just a small sample of what we're talking about, take a look at the exclusive preview pages that start on page 349. [Hey, did you know the Stan was a big Hardy Boys fan when he was a kid? It's true!]

They say life sometimes goes in cycles. Nearly ten years ago PH Marcondes started working for Papercutz on a graphic novel featuring a runaway train. In the second THE ZODIAC LEGACY graphic novel, coming out soon, PH Marcondes illustrates "Power Lines," an all-new graphic novel featuring teenagers with powers based on the signs of the Chinese zodiac, and it all takes place on a runaway train! That's in THE ZODIAC LEGACY #2, the preview in a few pages is of THE ZODIAC LEGACY #1.

It's funny. This special expanded edition of Watch Out for Papercutz is starting to feel like the special bonus features you get when you buy a boxed set of DVDs of a season's worth of a TV series. Lots of behind-the-scenes info, a special preview, and now a special bonus—a four-page outtake from "To Die or Not to Die?" It turns out that there's no such thing as miniature golf in Brazil, so when PH got the script for the opening sequence he was a little confused. Look at the next four pages to see how PH originally drew the start of "To Die or Not to Die?" It could've been called "Danger is Par for the (Biggest Miniature Golf) Course"!

Over the years, Papercutz has moved away from creating faux manga and has been publishing graphic novels featuring many of the world's most popular characters as well as new, original characters. We still get many requests to do more HARDY BOYS and NANCY DREW graphic novels. We will continue to publish collections of our past graphic novels, but if you're looking for all-new comics, allow me to direct you to comics publisher Dynamite. They will be launching new series starring Nancy Drew and Frank and Joe Hardy, and I suspect they'll be great. But in the meantime, be sure to check out the next volume of HARDY BOYS ADVENTURES—we're sure it'll be a blast! (See pic on the left!)

Thanks, JIM

DID YOU KNOW THEY DON'T HAVE MINIATURE GOLF IN BRAZIL? PH HAD NEVER EXPERIENCED MINI-GOLF WHEN HE RECEIVED INSTRUCTIONS TO ILLUSTRATE THIS SCENE.

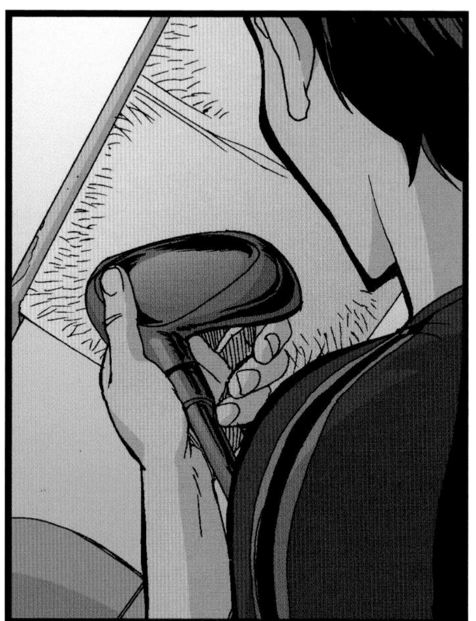

See how these pages were meant to appear in "To Die or Not to Die?" elsewhere in this graphic novel.

Special Preview of THE ZODIAC LEGACY #1 "Tiger Island" by Stan Lee, Stuart Moore, and PH Marcondes...

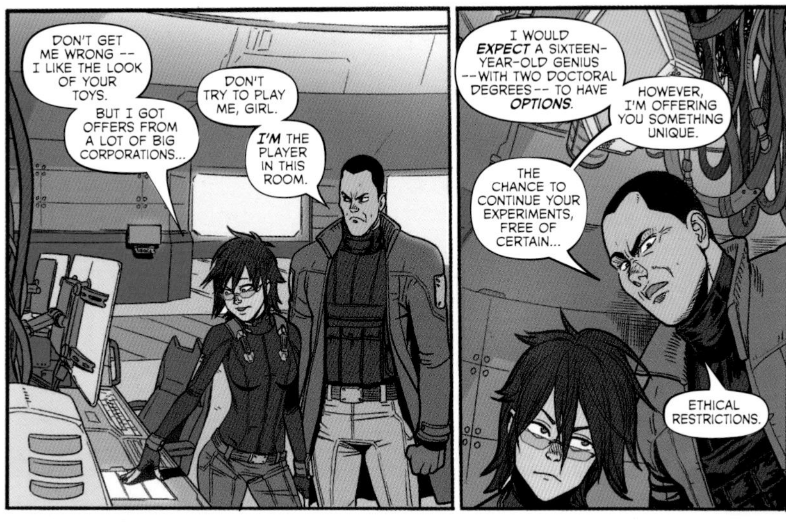
DON'T GET ME WRONG -- I LIKE THE LOOK OF YOUR TOYS.
BUT I GOT OFFERS FROM A LOT OF BIG CORPORATIONS...
DON'T TRY TO PLAY ME, GIRL.
I'M THE PLAYER IN THIS ROOM.
I WOULD EXPECT A SIXTEEN-YEAR-OLD GENIUS --WITH TWO DOCTORAL DEGREES-- TO HAVE OPTIONS.
HOWEVER, I'M OFFERING YOU SOMETHING UNIQUE.
THE CHANCE TO CONTINUE YOUR EXPERIMENTS, FREE OF CERTAIN...
ETHICAL RESTRICTIONS.

THAT'S TEMPTING.
BUT I GOTTA TELL YOU, MAN: ALL THIS ZODIAC STUFF SOUNDS PRETTY NUTS.
I DON'T WANT TO WORK FOR A CRAZY MAN, YOU KNOW?

HA! YOU'RE LUCKY I'M NOT EASILY OFFENDED.
PERHAPS IF I EXPLAIN FURTHER. VERY FEW PEOPLE IN THIS WORLD KNOW THE TRUTH...

...ABOUT *THE ZODIAC LEGACY.*
IT BEGAN ONE YEAR AGO. AFTER MANY YEARS OF SEARCHING, I FINALLY TRACKED A MASSIVE, ANCIENT ENERGY SOURCE...

"...TO A CAVERN FAR BENEATH THE CITY OF HONG KONG.
"THERE I FOUND TWELVE MYSTERIOUS POOLS... GLOWING WITH POWER.
"WITH THE AID OF A BRILLIANT SCIENTIST NAMED ***CARLOS***, I PREPARED FOR ***THE CONVERGENCE:*** THE ONE MOMENT IN 144 YEARS WHEN THE ZODIAC POWER COULD BE CONCENTRATED AND AMPLIFIED.

"MY PLAN WAS TO ABSORB THE POWER OF ALL TWELVE ZODIAC SIGNS INTO ***MYSELF*** -- TEMPORARILY. THEN I WOULD PASS IT ALONG TO AGENTS IN MY EMPLOY."

EXCEPT FOR THE ***DRAGON***-- THE MOST POWERFUL SIGN OF THEM ALL.
THAT WAS TO BE ***MINE.***

"BUT I HADN'T FORESEEN CARLOS'S TREACHERY.
"AFTER I'D ABSORBED SEVERAL OF THE POWERS, CARLOS TURNED AGAINST ME.
HE SABOTAGED THE CONVERGENCE, CAUSING THE ZODIAC ENERGIES TO RUN WILD.
"CARLOS'S ACCOMPLICE WAS A FORMER EMPLOYEE OF MINE: *JASMINE.*
"LIKE ME, SHE IS A DRAGON. AND AS THE CONVERGENCE CHAMBER EXPLODED INTO CHAOS, SHE MANAGED TO STEAL SOME OF THE DRAGON ENERGY FOR HERSELF.
"STILL: EVEN WITH HALF THE DRAGON'S POWER, I MIGHT HAVE BEEN ABLE TO SALVAGE THE SITUATION.
"HAD IT NOT BEEN FOR ANOTHER UNTIMELY ARRIVAL: